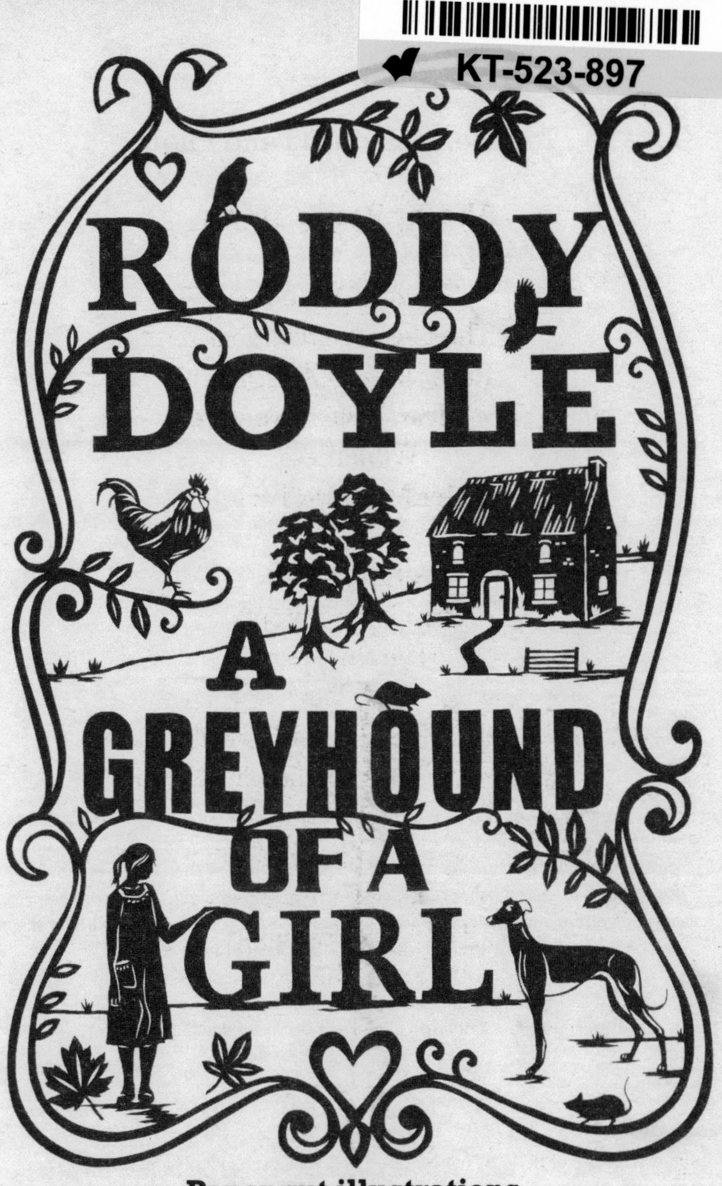

Paper cut illustrations
Julene Harrison

To Kate, Belinda, Ita and Ellen

First published in the UK in 2011 by Marion Lloyd Books
An imprint of Scholastic Children's Books
Euston House, 24 Eversholt Street
London, NW1 1DB, UK
A division of Scholastic Ltd.
Registered office: Westfield Road, Southam, Warwickshire, CV47 0RA

ISBN 9781407130156

A CIP catalogue record for this book is available from the British Library

Printed by CPI Bookmarque Ltd, Croydon, Surrey
Papers used by Scholastic Children's Books are made from wood grown in sustainable forests.

1 3 5 7 9 10 8 6 4 2

www.scholastic.co.uk/zone

She hated the hospital. She hated walking through it. She hated everything about it.

Except for one thing. Her granny.

She hated the hospital but she loved her granny.

Mary O'Hara was walking up her street, to the house she lived in with her parents and her brothers. The school bus had dropped her at the corner, at the bottom of the hill. The street was long, straight and quite steep, and there were huge, old chestnut trees growing all along both sides. It was raining but Mary wasn't getting very wet, because the leaves and branches were like a roof above her. Anyway, rain and getting wet were things that worried adults, but not Mary – or anyone else under the age of twenty-one. Mary was twelve. She'd be twelve for another eight months. Then she'd be what she already felt she was – a teenager.

She came home at the same time most days and she usually came home with her best friend, Ava. But today was different, because Ava wasn't with Mary. Ava had moved to another part of Dublin the day before, with her family. Today, some of the neighbours looked out their windows and saw Mary, alone. They knew all about it, of course. These were people who looked out windows. They'd seen the removals lorry outside Ava's house. They'd seen Mary and Ava hug each other, and they'd seen Ava get into their car and follow the removals lorry. As the car moved slowly up the street, they'd seen Mary wave, and run into her house. They might have heard the front door slam. They might have heard Mary's feet charging up the stairs, and the springs under Mary's mattress groan when she fell face down on the bed. They probably didn't hear her crying, and they definitely didn't hear the softer sound of the bed springs a little later when Mary realized that, although she was heartbroken, she was also starving. So she got up and went downstairs to the kitchen and ate until her face was stiff.

Today, Mary walked alone, up the hill. She was nearly home. There were just a few houses left before she got to hers. There was a gap between the trees for a while, so the raindrops fell on her. But she didn't notice them, or care.

Someone had once told her that people who'd had their legs cut off still felt the leg, even a long time after they'd lost them. They felt an itch and went to scratch, and remembered that there was no leg there. That was how Mary felt. She felt Ava walking beside her. She knew she wasn't, but she looked anyway – and that made it worse.

Mary knew: Ava was somewhere else in Dublin, only seven kilometres away. But if she'd been acting in a film or a play and she was told she had to cry, she'd have thought of Ava and crying would have been easy. Feeling angry and looking angry would have been easy too. Mary couldn't understand why people moved house. It was stupid. And she couldn't understand why parents – Ava's parents – said No when two friends – Mary and Ava – asked if it was okay if one of them – Ava – didn't move but, instead, lived with the other friend – Mary.

"You won't have to feed her if she lives with us," Mary had told Ava's mother the day before they'd moved. "It'll, like, save you a fortune."

"No."

"Especially with the recession and that."

"No."

"Why not?" Ava asked.

"Because you're our daughter and we love you."

"Then do the noble thing and let her stay," said Mary. "If you, like, really, really love her. It's not funny."

"I know," said Ava's mother. "It's just so sweet."

Which was exactly the sort of stupid thing that adults said. They saw two best friends clinging to each other, wanting to die rather than be separated – and they said it was sweet.

"I suppose you think war and starvation are sweet too, like, do you?" said Mary.

"You're being a little bit rude, Mary," said Ava's mother.

"Whatever," said Mary.

She stood at Ava's front door. Then she tried to slam it. But she couldn't. There was a thick rug in the hall, and it seemed to grab the bottom of the door. So, she'd shouted it instead.

"Slam!"

And she'd stormed off to her own house where the slamming was easier.

"That's a wet one."

Someone had just spoken to Mary. But she couldn't see anyone. She was alone on the street, just outside her house.

Then she saw the woman.

She must have been behind one of the trees, Mary thought.

The woman was old. But, actually, she wasn't. Mary knew what it was, why the woman seemed old. She was old-fashioned. She was wearing a dress that looked like it came from an old film, one of those films her mother always cried at. She looked like a woman who milked cows and threw hay with a pitchfork. She was even wearing big boots with fat laces.

A bird above them must have flown away quickly, because the leaves shook and dropped loads of water on to their heads. Mary laughed – she felt the raindrops this time – but the woman didn't seem to notice. Nothing about her was wet. But—

"It's a wet one, alright," she said. "Did you get loads of homework, did you?"

"The usual," said Mary.

"What's the usual when it's at home?"

Mary laughed again. The woman sounded like her grandmother. But, then, that made her sad, and angry again. She was going to cry – she thought she was.

"What's wrong with you?" said the woman.

"My granny's not well," said Mary.

"Sure, I know," said the woman.

"Well, why did you ask then?" said Mary.

"God, you're a rip, alright."

"What does that mean?"

"You're a cheeky young lady," said the woman.

"Everyone says that," said Mary. "That I'm cheeky. But I'm not. I'm just honest."

"Good girl yourself."

Mary looked at the woman again. She wasn't old at all. She looked younger than Mary's mother, although it was hard to tell with adults what age they were. Mary was sure she'd never seen this woman before.

Never talk to strangers, she'd always been told.

"But that's stupid," she'd said, a few years ago.

"Why is it stupid?" her mother asked.

"Did you know Dad when you met him?" said Mary.

"No."

"So he was a stranger."

"But—"

"And you spoke to him," said Mary. "So if, like, nobody spoke to strangers, nobody would meet and get married and the human race would, like, cease to exist."

"But your dad wasn't a stranger."

"Yes, he was. He must have been."

"He wasn't strange," said her mother. "He was nice."

"Nice?" said Mary. "The nice fellas are the ones you should be worried about."

Her mother laughed.

"What's so funny?" said Mary.

"Who told you that?"

"Granny."

"I should have known," said her mother. "Well, never mind your granny."

"Don't talk to strangers, never mind your granny," said Mary. "I'll have no one left to talk to."

"But you know what I mean," said her mother.

"About strangers?"

"Yes."

"Don't worry," said Mary. "I won't talk to any."

But she did – now.

"How do you know about my granny?" she asked the woman.

"Ah sure, I just do," said the woman.

She stood back, and shimmered – kind of – as if she was stepping behind a sheet of clear plastic.

"It's life," she said – and she was solid again, and smiling.

But Mary was a bit scared, and cold.

"I have to go," she said.

"Right, so," said the woman.

She didn't step out of the way. She didn't seem to

move at all. But, even so, she must have, because she wasn't in front of Mary any more.

Mary walked quickly to her gate. She heard the woman behind her.

"Do one small thing for me, Mary."

Mary turned.

"Tell your granny it'll all be grand," said the woman – she was still smiling.

"How did you know my name?" Mary asked her.

"Sure, half the girls in Ireland are called Mary," said the woman.

"No, they aren't," said Mary. "I'm the only one on our road."

"Well, they were all called Mary in my day," said the woman. "Off you go, so. I'll see you the next time."

The next time? Mary should have been worried, even frightened. She *was* worried, and a bit frightened. But not nearly as much as she thought she should have been. This woman had come out of nowhere. She knew Mary's name and all about her granny – Mary should have been terrified. But she wasn't. Something about the woman, the way she spoke, her face, her smile – she seemed familiar. Mary didn't know her – but she *did*.

She wasn't terrified. But, still, she ran to the front door and rang the bell instead of getting her key from her school bag. As she rang the bell she turned. But the woman had gone.

She heard the door opening.

"Mary!"

It was her mother.
"How was school?!"
"Stupid."
She went straight past her mother, into the hall.
"What's your hurry?!"
"I'm starving."

Losing your best friend was heartbreaking but some things about it weren't too bad. So far, Mary had been promised new jeans, two new tops, a trip to the cinema, and French toast for her lunch two days in a row.

There was no smell of French toast when her mother opened the door but that was okay, because Mary was the one who was going to make it. She'd decided to become a chef.

"Great idea!" said her mother.

"Stop talking like that," said Mary.

"Like what?!"

"Like !!!!!!!!!!!!"

"Oh, no!" said her mother, whose name was Scarlett. "I don't talk like that! Do I?!"

"Yes, you do."

"What?! Always?!"

"Yes!"

"I'm sorry!" Scarlett whispered.

"Even your whispers end in !!!s," Mary whispered back.

"You said you wanted to be a chef."

"That's right."

"A world famous chef, I think you said."

"Right again."

"So, what do you concentrate on first?! 'World', or 'famous', or 'chef'?!"

This was the kind of question Mary loved, so she gave it some thought.

"Chef," she said, after about ten seconds.

"I think you're right!" said Scarlett.

"I know I am," said Mary. "You have to be a chef before you can be a famous one."

"Yes!"

"The same way, like, I'd have to murder someone if I wanted to become a world famous murderer," said Mary. "Not that I'm looking at anyone in particular."

Cheekiness was often a sign of intelligence. So Scarlett usually liked it when Mary was being cheeky. *My brainy daughter has insulted me yet again!* Sometimes, though, it was just tiring, and even Mary's snores sounded cheeky.

"Oh, shut up, Mary!" said Scarlett.

And Mary did. Because, if cheekiness was often a sign of intelligence, so was keeping your mouth shut.

The plan was, Mary would cook something different

every day and what she cooked would gradually become more complicated. They'd made a list, ten days' worth of cooking. Scarlett loved lists – but Mary kept her mouth shut.

Now, today, just after she'd met the woman outside, Mary walked down the hall to the kitchen.

"You seem a bit more cheerful!" said Scarlett.

Normally, that comment would have really annoyed Mary, her mother trying to force her to be happy. But, just as she got ready to tell her mother that, No, she wasn't more cheerful, she realized something: she actually was more cheerful.

So she closed her mouth, and started again.

"I suppose I am," she said.

"Great!" said Scarlett. "So school was okay!"

"No," said Mary.

"Oh!" said Scarlett. "But you had fun on the bus home!"

"No."

"Well, I bet you're hungry."

"No," said Mary. "I mean, yeah. I'm starving, like. But that's not why I feel better. Starving people don't feel better."

"Why then?!" said Scarlett.

Mary was already cracking the eggs, on the side of a glass bowl.

"I met our new neighbour," she said. "She's nice."

"What new neighbour?!" Scarlett asked. "Have they moved into Ava's house already?"

She got out of the way while Mary whisked the eggs.

Mary's hand was a blur and specks of egg yolk were hitting the wall, like yellow flies committing suicide.

"No," said Mary. "Ava's house looks empty. She's in a different one, I think. She's old."

"Old?"

"I mean, she isn't old," said Mary.

She'd finished whisking, and most of the egg was still in the bowl.

"She talked old, like," she said. "But, actually, I'd say she was as young as you. Maybe younger."

"She talked old?!"

"Yeah," said Mary. "Old-fashioned, like. Like Granny. And she dressed old too. In a dress and stuff."

"I don't think I've seen her," said Scarlett.

Mary had added milk and salt to the egg. She lowered the first slice of bread into the mixture.

"What's her name?" said Scarlett.

"Don't know," said Mary.

She put the frying pan on top of the cooker and turned on the gas. She loved the whoosh the gas made when it sparked, and she loved the blue colour of the flame. It was much more interesting than red. She dropped the butter on to the pan and watched it melt and start to fizzle. Then she lowered the first slice of egg-and-milk-soaked bread.

"I'll ask her the next time," she said. "She's nice. And so is this French toast."

The first slice was for Scarlett.

"Thank you!" she said. "It's lovely!"

"Eat it first," said Mary. "Then tell me."

"I am! It's even lovelier!"

They ate three slices each.

"Ready?!" Scarlett asked, as she dropped the plates and cutlery into the sink. She tried to sound even more enthusiastic than usual. But Mary's mother hated this part of the day – this journey that had shoved itself into their routine every day for the past five weeks – just as much as Mary hated it.

"Okay," said Mary.

Mary didn't like the hospital. She hated the smell of the place, and the noise, and the people in the corridors crying and holding each other, and the sick people in their dressing gowns at the front door, smoking and coughing. The place frightened her. Even the name, Sacred Heart Hospital, scared her a bit. The Sacred Heart, people called it. *She's in the Sacred Heart*. Mary imagined a huge bloody heart with a squelchy door that you had to squeeze through, and blood dripping from the ceiling. She knew it was silly. The hospital was actually a grey building that didn't drip blood at all, although water leaked in one of the corridors. But there were all sorts of warnings about swine flu, or H1N1, and winter vomiting and coughing and sanitizers and washing your hands and paying your bills, all over the walls and doors. She hated it, not because she was afraid she'd catch the swine flu or that she'd start vomiting on the first day of winter. It was the atmosphere of the place – all the sickness and warnings. Mary loved her granny but she didn't like having to go to see her – and that made her feel bad too.

Her granny was very sick, but also very cheerful. Her smile got bigger and wider when she saw Mary.

"Get up here beside me," she said.

"Okay," said Mary.

She took off her boots and climbed up on the bed and lay down beside her granny.

"Oh my, Granny," said Mary. "What big teeth you have."

It was a Mary-Granny joke that went back to the time when Granny had first read her *Little Red Riding Hood*, when Mary was only five. (Although Mary's granny's teeth actually were quite big.)

Her granny smiled again.

"All the better to eat you with, my dear," she said.

"Start at my feet," said Mary.

"They're too far away," said her granny. "You're growing too fast."

"I know," said Mary. "I'm really good at growing."

"She'll be as tall as you, Mum!" said Scarlett.

"Like all of us," said Mary's granny – Scarlett's mother. "We're all tall girls."

"How are you feeling today?" Mary asked.

"Ah sure," said her granny. "I've felt better. My own

growing days are over. But, sure, the bed is grand and comfy. What did you do in school today?"

"Nothing."

"Nothing?" said her granny. "That was my favourite subject. I was always good at doing nothing. Top of the class, every blessed time."

Then she fell asleep. And that was frightening too, how quickly, how easily her granny fell – *dropped* – into sleep. It was always so sudden, as if she'd been unplugged, no yawn or smile, just the sudden drop.

Mary kissed her granny's forehead. Then she climbed back down off the bed. Scarlett kissed the forehead too. And Granny's eyes opened.

"I'm frightened, Scarlett," she said, very quietly.

"It's fine," said Scarlett.

"I'm afraid I'll never open my eyes again."

"I know," said Scarlett. "But you opened them this time."

"That's true," said her mother. "I'm not dead yet."

"No," said Scarlett, and she smiled. "You're not."

"Here goes," said Granny.

And she shut her eyes.

She opened them.

"Just checking."

She closed them.

"Go on," she said. "I'm fine. I'm too lively to die today."

Her eyes stayed closed. They watched her breathing, a little smile on her old face. She was asleep.

They left.

"What's actually wrong with Granny?" Mary asked, on the way home in the car.

"Nothing really," said her mother. "She's very old, you know. No one lives forever."

"Why not?"

Her mother looked at Mary.

"We just don't," she said. "We're mortal. You know what that means."

"Yeah," said Mary. "But it just seems mean."

"You're right," said her mother. "It does seem mean. Especially when it's someone you love."

They cried. And they laughed a bit too, because they were crying.

"Oh dear," said her mother. "I can hardly see the road ahead of me."

"What happened the !!!s?" said Mary.

"What?"

"The !!!s," said Mary.

"Oh," said her mother. "They seem to fall out of me whenever I go into that hospital."

When they got back to the house, Mary's brothers had come home from their school.

"Hi, boys!"

"They're back," said Mary.

"The boys?!"

"No, the !!!s."

"Oh, good!"

The boys were back but Mary didn't care. Her brothers were older than her. At 14 and 16, they were boring and weird. They used to be Dominic and Kevin but these days they preferred to be called Dommo and Killer. They had deep voices that made all the cups in the kitchen shake and their bedroom and most of the house smelled of a deodorant called Lynx that made Mary's eyes water whenever she strolled through a cloud of it. They laughed a lot and never explained why.

It was an hour later, and Mary was having her dinner with Dommo and Killer, and her mother and father, whose name was Paddy.

The boys were laughing, and nudging each other.

"What's so funny?" asked Paddy.

"Nothing," said Dommo.

"Is there any ice-cream?" asked Killer.

"It's a weekday!" said Scarlett. "What's so funny?!"

"Nothing."

"Laughing at nothing," said Paddy. "I'd love to see the state of yis when you're laughing at something."

This time, they didn't laugh.

"I give up," said Paddy.

They laughed.

"How was your mother?" Paddy asked Scarlett.

"Fine," she said. "Not fine. The usual. God, it feels cruel just talking about it."

The boys weren't laughing. They loved their grandmother. She'd always called them her mad fellas, for as long as they could remember. She'd listened to everything they'd ever said, every whinge and complaint, and always answered the same way: "You're dead right." And she'd always greeted them the same way, from the time Dommo was five and Killer was three: "Any girlfriends yet, lads?" They'd only been to the hospital once and they'd spent all the time there showing their granny how to use their iPods. They had to show her how to put in the earphones. She tried to sit up straight. She held an iPod in both her hands.

"Give me a listen to these lads here," she shouted – she read the name. "The Kings of Leon."

She'd listened to about thirty seconds of one song.

"Not too bad," she shouted. "But they're not a patch on Elvis."

"D'you like Elvis, Granny?" said Dommo.

"What?!"

"D'you like Elvis?"

"Love him!" she shouted.

"Did you ever see him?" Killer asked.

"No, I did not," she shouted. "He never came to our parish. But, sure, boys, I'll be meeting him soon enough."

They'd laughed, because she'd wanted them to, even though she'd been talking about her own death. But it was nothing new, really. She'd always made them laugh. Just like Mary, they hated the hospital, and they hated the fact that they almost never went. They refused to go, because they hated it so much. They felt like cowards, although they'd never spoken about it. They missed their granny, they felt sorry for their mother, and for themselves. But they didn't know what to say, and they were too old for hugging. They were too old for everything.

But they stayed downstairs after dinner with Mary and their parents and they all watched *Ireland's Got Talent*.

"Well," said Paddy during the ads. "All I can say is, Ireland's got absolutely no talent."

The boys didn't laugh.

"I think it's good!" said Scarlett.

The boys laughed.

"The guy with the singing toothbrush was quite funny!"

The boys laughed.

"But did you see his teeth?" said Paddy. "They were rotten."

The boys didn't laugh.

"Why isn't that funny?" Paddy asked.

The boys shrugged.

"Just," said Killer.

"Just what?"

Killer shrugged.

They watched the rest of the show, three more acts: a woman who juggled three knives and left the stage early, whimpering and clutching her shoulder; a boy who spun on his head until he got sick, and a nun with a baseball cap who sang "Don't Stop Believing", in Irish.

When it was over, Paddy stretched his legs and arms. He yawned.

"Time for bed," he said. "What's so funny?"

"Nothing."

"It's too early for bed," said Killer.

"It's never too early for bed," said their father.

"That's just sad," said Dommo.

"I agree," said Paddy.

He stood up and handed the remote control to Dommo.

"Make sure you don't watch anything educational," he said.

They didn't laugh.

"It was *so* nice you watched telly with us, boys!" said Scarlett.

"Okay."

"Telly off in half an hour, okay."

"An hour."

"Three quarters."

"Goodnight!" said Scarlett. "I love you both!"

Dommo muttered something that sounded a little like "Uv U2", but Killer said nothing.

Mary didn't say goodnight to her brothers. She didn't know how. She didn't know them. She used to, but not any more. They'd changed into aliens. It worried her sometimes – a lot of the time. She worried that she'd turn into one of them. Dommo was only two years older than Mary, so she only had two years of normal life left, before she'd start grunting and laughing at nothing. Unless the weird stuff only happened to boys. She knew all about her own body and what was going to be happening soon, but that didn't worry her – at all. It excited her, all the changes just around the corner. It wasn't the changes to her body that scared or worried Mary. It was the stranger ones, the ones that had turned her brothers into strangers. She didn't want to be like them. She thought they were probably lonely.

But, then, so was she.

She changed into the clothes she liked for bed, a hoodie and pyjama bottoms. Then she went to the bathroom and brushed her teeth. She had one of her baby teeth left, the only person in her class with any. It was at the back and it was loose, so she nudged it a bit. The dentist had told her to do this, every morning and every night.

"Come out or I'll kill you," she said to her mouth in the mirror.

Threatening the tooth was her own idea, not the dentist's. She gave up and went to her parents' bedroom. She looked in at them sitting up, reading.

"Did you brush your teeth?" she asked.

"Yes!"

"Yeah."

This was an old routine, repeated every night – *every* night. Mary would ask the stupid adult questions and her parents would give the child's answers. They'd been doing it for years, ever since Mary had read her father a bedtime story one night and they'd laughed so much, because it had seemed so silly, that they'd done it again the night after, and the one after that. Until, even when her parents weren't going to bed, they pretended they were, for the fun.

"Did both of you brush them?"

"Yes!"

"Smell my breath if you want to."

"No, thank you," said Mary. "Night night."

She kissed them both on the forehead.

"Lights out in a few minutes, okay?"

"Aw!"

"Okay."

As she walked to the door and went out to the landing, she suddenly knew something: soon she'd stop doing what she'd just done. She just knew, one day she wouldn't want to do it any more. And that made her sad.

She got into bed and felt all alone. She was tempted to go back to her parents, but she stayed where she was. She read a bit of her book, *Twilight*. But she was tired and not even the story – it was the best book she'd ever read and she'd seen the film seven times – could keep her awake. She turned off the bedside light and lay back and almost immediately she was asleep.

Mary never closed her curtains. She liked the different lights that came through the window at night, especially the shadows made by the swaying leaves and the beams of cars that raced across her ceiling. She often fell asleep counting cars. So she kept the curtains open. And tonight this was interesting because the woman Mary had met earlier was sitting outside, on the window sill.

"What's your name?" Mary asked.

"Tansey," said the woman.

It was the day after the first time they'd met, and the woman was suddenly there again, walking beside Mary, in the same dress and the same big boots. The boots were mucky, but the muck looked clean and shining, as if the boots had been painted to look mucky. There she was, and Mary suddenly remembered that they'd met the day before. She'd completely forgotten.

"Tansey?" said Mary. "Is it, like, short for something?"

"It is," said the woman.

"Well," said Mary. "What is it short for?"

"Anastasia."

Mary stopped walking, and looked at the woman – Anastasia. The name seemed old-fashioned too, like everything else about her. She was smiling at Mary. It was cold but she wasn't wearing a jacket or even a jumper.

"I've heard that name before," said Mary.

"Sure, it's only a name," said the woman.

"I suppose," said Mary. "Have you moved into Ava's house?"

"I have not," said the woman. "And who's Ava when she's at home?"

"My friend," said Mary. "And she's not at home. She moved."

"Oh dear."

"It's stupid," said Mary.

"You're dead right, girl."

"Which house do you live in then?"

"I don't," said Tansey.

"What?"

"I don't live in any house at all."

Mary was nervous – again. Was the woman mad? Or even dangerous? But Mary looked at the woman's face and she became calm. There was nothing mad or dangerous there. She was smiling and there was a tiny wrinkle beside one of her eyes that looked a bit like an extra smile.

"I know," said Mary. "You live in one of the apartments."

She pointed at the grey and red block at the end of the street.

"No, I do not," said Tansey. "What's an apartment?"

She put her hands on top of a garden wall and lifted herself on to it. She did it quickly and easily; she didn't groan or gasp. She sat there like it was a perfectly natural thing for an adult to do.

"Up you get now," she said to Mary, and she patted the place beside her.

Mary took her school bag off her back and jumped at the wall. She was a good climber, although she didn't really do that kind of thing any more. It was ages since she'd climbed a wall. She couldn't remember the last time.

She sat beside the woman.

"Which do you prefer?" she asked.

"What?"

"Tansey or Anastasia?"

"Oh," said the woman, "I was always Tansey. No one ever called me Anastasia."

She spoke like Mary's granny sometimes did, as if she was remembering something, even seeing something, that had happened long ago, or far away.

"It took too long, I suppose," said Tansey. "Sure, I'd be gone before they got to the end of that name. Ana-stay-zeeee-aaaahh. I'd be halfway to Gorey on my bike."

She smiled at Mary.

"Isn't this nice now."

"Yeah," said Mary.

"Will you be seeing your granny today, will you?" the woman asked.

"Yeah," said Mary. "I think."

"Did you give her that message yesterday," said the woman.

"What message?"

"I told you to tell her that it'll all be grand."

"I forgot," said Mary.

The woman looked annoyed, for half a second. It was strange: her face went back to normal, but the annoyed expression was right behind it, as if two masks, happy and sad, had been brought together, to make one mask. Then the annoyed – the sad – look was gone and she was smiling again. The wrinkle at her eye deepened and became part of her smile.

"You'll remember it today," she said.

"Yeah," said Mary.

"Tell her Tansey told you."

"Does Granny know you?"

"She does," said the woman. "She *did*. Well, I suppose you have homework, do you?"

"Yeah," sighed Mary.

"You poor suffering creature," said the woman. "You'd better go inside and do it, so."

"Okay," said Mary.

"The same time tomorrow?" said the woman. "Will you be strolling past at all?"

Mary laughed. She loved the way the woman talked. She'd forgotten that she'd been nervous only a minute before. And she'd forgotten that she still didn't know where the woman lived.

She jumped off the wall and picked up her bag.

"I will be strolling past at all," she said as she walked away, trying to sound like the woman.

She looked back, to see if the woman had noticed, or cared. But the woman wasn't there.

Or, she was.

It was like a television screen in sunlight. The woman's dress, all of the woman, had faded, become colourless. Then, quickly, as if a curtain had been closed to block the light or the sun had gone behind a cloud, the woman and her colours were sharp again and definitely there.

Mary looked up: the sun *had* gone behind a cloud.

"Bye, so," said Mary.

"Bye bye," said the woman.

Mary walked away and, again, she looked back.

"I'm still here," said the woman. "The long stuff today, is it? You're having for your dinner."

Mary thought for a while.

"Spaghetti," she said. She'd remembered: spaghetti was what she'd be cooking today, on day two of her campaign to become a chef.

"Is that what it's called?" said the woman.

Mary laughed.

"That's what it's called," she said.

"It looks like quare stuff," said the woman.

"It's lovely."

"See you tomorrow, so," said the woman.

"See you tomorrow, so, so," said Mary.

She walked the rest of the way to her front door and didn't look back. She took her key from her bag and let herself in.

"Mary!"

"Hi."

"How was school?"

"Stupid."

Spaghetti bolognaise was easy enough to cook. Her mother showed Mary a trick. She took a piece of spaghetti from the boiling water, with a fork.

"Now, watch!"

She took the spaghetti off the fork and held it for a second. Then she threw it at the wall. It stuck there.

"It's ready!" said Scarlett.

Mary laughed.

"How do you know?"

"Just throw it at the wall!" said Scarlett. "If it sticks, it's done! If it doesn't, you're either too late or too early!"

The bolognaise sauce came out of a jar.

"Are we, like, not supposed to make it?" Mary asked.

"Well, yes!" said Scarlett. "Strictly speaking! But there's a knack to pouring sauce from a jar too! It's a skill you have to learn! Oh, well done, Mary!"

Mary had just poured the sauce into the pot without spilling any.

"Nothing to it," she said.

She started to stir in the sauce. The spaghetti felt heavy, as if it was putting up a fight.

"It's quare stuff," she said.

Scarlett laughed.

"More Granny-talk!" she said.

"How did she know it was going to be spaghetti?" Mary asked herself, out loud.

"Who?!" said Scarlett. "Granny?!"

"No," said Mary. "The woman. Tansey."

She was still fighting with the spaghetti, making sure all the sauce got in among the strands. So she didn't realize that the kitchen was suddenly silent. She stopped stirring – her wrist was beginning to ache – and then she noticed.

"What's wrong?"

Her mother looked pale. Her mouth was hanging open, a bit.

"Tansey?" she said.

"Yeah," said Mary. "Why?"

"Who is she?"

"The new woman," said Mary. "I told you about her yesterday, like. I think I did."

"Yes," said Scarlett. "You did. You met her again today, did you?"

"Yeah," said Mary. "She's nice. She's funny."

"Sorry," said Scarlett. "It was the name."

"What about it?"

"You never hear it these days."

Mary watched her mother. She waited for her to speak again.

"Your great-grandmother," said Scarlett. "Granny's mother. She was called Tansey."

The morning's work was nearly over, all the jobs that had to be done around the farm. But really, Tansey knew, that idea – morning's work – meant nothing. There was the dinner to be made for when Jim and the other men came in from the fields and then there were the jobs that would have to be done this afternoon, right into the evening and night, right up to the side of the bed. It was one long day of work.

But she loved it. On a day like today, Tansey loved everything she had to do. It was early spring, and the muck was still hard. She loved walking across it. She could feel its ridges through her boots. She'd just been getting the eggs out from under the chickens. She had a basket full of the lads and she'd be taking them into Enniscorthy tomorrow morning, when Jim was bringing the milk to the creamery. She'd go with him, up on the cart behind the donkey. It was something to look forward to, the shopping, the bit of chat. She'd buy herself a bag of boiled sweets. Jim's mother would look after Emer and the little lad, James the Baby, while she was gone.

Emer was running ahead of her now, holding one of the eggs in both her hands. She'd had the flu. She'd been up in the bed for more than two weeks, and they'd been frightened for a few days and nights, with the heat that had come off her. But she was grand now, fully recovered; there wasn't a bother on her. She was charging ahead there, dying to get back to the house to show the egg to her granny.

"Hegg!"

She was shouting already, announcing her arrival. Tansey could see Emer's breath, like a little cloud sailing ahead of her. Their morning breath came out in steam but it wasn't cold. It was one of those days, like an announcement. The sky was extra blue; the lambs down in the far field sounded as if they were right beside her. Winter was over. It would still be bright when they'd be bringing the cows in for the evening milking. Emer was wearing her coat but, soon enough, they'd hang it up on the hook and it wouldn't come back down till the other end of the year.

Emer would be three next week. On the Tuesday, that would be. Tansey would get the ingredients for the sweet-cake tomorrow when she was doing the shop. And Emer would be able to help her make it.

That would be lovely, the first real time they'd bake together.

Everything was lovely on a day like this one.

She'd make the dinner now. Jim's mother would already be at it; the spuds would be on, boiling away. There were eight mouths to feed. She'd do more of the churning after the dinner, after they'd cleaned the kitchen. She'd bring the butter to the creamery tomorrow, and someone in Enniscorthy or even up in Dublin would be putting it on their toast or spuds in a few days' time. The churning was a hard oul' job but then there was the result, the satisfaction. The butter. There was nothing like it. Jim had carved a beautiful T on to each of the butter paddles, so that her sign – T for Tansey – was on every pound of butter that she made. That was a great thing. She felt like a writer with her name on the cover of a book. Jim had given her the paddles at Christmas. Blushing he was, grinning, like a handsome big child.

She loved that man, her husband. And he loved her. She saw that every time he looked at her. Every time she caught him looking. Her husband. She still wasn't really used to that – even though they'd be married four years in April and they already had two children, Emer and James the Baby. The 11th of April, 1924. That was the day she stopped being Tansey Wallace and she became Anastasia Mary Stafford. Anastasia just for the big day, and Tansey Stafford after that.

She'd feed the greyhounds before she went in. She opened the gate to their pen. Emer had run ahead with her egg, into the house. She didn't like the dogs.

"Too bony!" she said.

And she had a point. They were skinny creatures, the hounds, too bony for petting. Emer loved the old sheepdog, Parnell. He lay beside the fire all day, too deaf now to hear the sheep or care where they were off to. But Tansey liked the hounds. Their pointy snouts rubbed against her hands. They knew she'd be feeding them, so all seven of them were trailing after her.

"Sure, it's nice to be wanted," she told them.

There'd be no food for the hounds tomorrow because Jim had them racing in Enniscorthy and he'd want them hungry to go after the hare. The ground was soft in here. She checked again, but it was grand: she'd remembered to put the latch on the gate. This corner got the early sun; there was no skin on the muck. She'd have to wash her boots. But that was grand too. It was one of those days; there'd be no ache when she bent down to take them off. No amount of work would make her feel anything but young. Tansey was 25, and on a day like today you could add the word *only* to that: Tansey Stafford was *only* 25.

The hounds were fed and happy. Tansey put the latch on the gate and headed for the house. She was hungry herself now. There'd be a new thatch going up on the roof in September. The decision had been made; the money was there for the job. The old thatch had been up there since before the hungry years, since the days when Jim's mother's mother was a child. There were mice up in that thatch that had never seen the light of day. One of them fell on to her lap one night, and her sitting at the fire, trying to see the hole in a sock that she was darning. A tiny little lad, but, all the same, it gave her a great big fright. The scream was out of her before she could call it back. It startled Emer out of her sleep and even made the baby jump, and him not even born yet, still snoozing away inside her. She'd felt like an eejit, especially when she saw the size of the poor creature that had fallen out of his home above. But Tansey had grown up in a house with slates. Her daddy was a policeman; she'd lived in whatever barracks he'd been sent to. Until she'd got the job in the drapery in Gorey, when she was 17, and she'd lived in a room above the shop with another girl, Eileen. Then she'd met Jim, when she slid on the ice outside the church and he was there just a little too late to catch her but just in time to pick her up.

"Were you deliberately slow?" she'd asked him later, when they'd become an item and everyone knew they'd be getting married.

"I was," he said. "You'd a lovely way of falling. It was like a show."

"It's just as well," she'd said. "If I hadn't fallen you wouldn't have asked me was I alright and I wouldn't have said I was and, sure, that's how it all started."

"It was worth the bruises, so, was it?"

"Sure, I never looked to see if there were bruises."

That was the way they were. They were easy with each other from the start, the best of friends before they knew what each other was called. Tansey would have thanked the ice if it hadn't melted.

She stood at the door. She always did, before she went in further. It was like walking into blackness if she didn't hesitate for a small moment. She took off the muddy boots while she was waiting for her eyes to catch up. She felt a bit of a chill now, sudden, like cold, wet fingers across her face. So she went on into the kitchen. It was full of the smells of bacon and cabbage and the cries of a child who had just dropped an egg.

She picked up Emer.

"What's the matter with you, at all?"

"The hegg!"

"You dropped it?"

"I did!"

"Ah, sure."

"It's dead."

"It's not dead, love. It's only smashed."

"I kilted it."

"No."

"I did!"

"No," said Tansey. "No. There's no life in an egg that isn't under its hen. And, sure, look it. We've a whole basket full of them. D'you want another one, do you?"

"No," said Emer.

"Suit yourself."

Emer was grand. Tansey could feel it in Emer's little body. The upset was out of her and the shock was becoming a memory. Tansey looked across at Jim's mother and saw that she didn't need any help yet. Tansey could sit at the fire with Emer on her lap. James the Baby was still asleep, wrapped up in the cot.

Tansey went across to the big chair with Emer still in her arms. The chair had been Jim's father's but Tansey had never known the man. He'd been dead for a year before she slid on the ice and met Jim. But, all the same, she felt she knew him, because a part of him – his tobacco, and the smells he'd brought in from the four corners of the farm – still seemed to be in the chair. He'd been a difficult man, by all accounts, and he'd told Jim not to bother looking for a wife while himself and Jim's mother were still walking the earth. *Two wives into one kitchen won't go*. But, difficult or not, she thought she'd have liked him. She always felt welcome when she decided to sit herself into the chair.

"It was only a hegg," said Emer.

"It was," said her mammy. "A fine class of an egg, mind, but only an egg."

She got her fingers to the buttons of Emer's coat and helped her take it off. She felt Emer wriggle a bit, so she could get out of the coat. All of Emer's fretting and upset came off with the coat. Tansey dropped it on to the floor, safe away from the ashes, and beside sleeping Parnell. She put her arms around Emer again.

"My dote," she said. "How are you now?"

"I'm grand," said Emer. "Close your eyes."

It was Emer's game. Tansey closed her eyes and waited. She felt Emer shift her weight on her lap. She felt Emer's lips touch her chin.

She spoke her line – it had to be the exact same; that was the rule.

"Ah now, I know that kiss."

She opened her eyes, wide as she could.

"It's Emer!"

Emer squealed and Tansey got ready to do it again. But suddenly – before it became a proper thought – she didn't feel too good. A sweat came to her forehead, and she thought she was going to be sick. She sat back and hoped the dizziness would fade. She closed her eyes.

Emer knew there was something wrong. Tansey could feel it in the child's restlessness. She wanted to open her eyes, to get on with the day she'd been loving. But she couldn't. She had to sleep.

She felt a hand, a cold hand, on her forehead.

"Oh Lord, the flu."

It was Jim's mother who spoke.

"Up to the bed with you, Tansey, girl."

"I'll be grand," said Tansey.

"Don't fight it," said Jim's mother. "And, of course, you'll be grand."

Tansey felt Emer being lifted from her. She heard the protest, the whimper. She opened her eyes but the room swam, so she shut them again and felt exhausted from the effort. She felt strong hands on her arm – Jim's mother's hands – and she tried to get out of the chair on her own steam. But she needed the help.

She was standing now, and shivering. But she opened her eyes and made sure she looked at Emer, and she smiled.

"Lucky me," she said. "Granny's bringing me up to the bed."

"Can I come with you?"

"Granny will need your help down here. Won't you, Granny?"

"Oh, I will," said Jim's mother. "I'd be hopeless without Emer."

The stairs was in the kitchen. The passage was narrow and steep. Tansey got up the first two steps and she turned and smiled at Emer. Then she kept going.

"Flu?"

"Yes."

"Swine flu?" said Mary.

"No, no," said her mother. "Ordinary flu."

"She, like, died of flu?"

"Yes," said Scarlett. "People often died of flu. Millions of people did. It was much more serious back then."

"When?"

"1928."

"That's so sad," said Mary.

"Yes, it is," said her mother. "And that's why I got a bit of a shock when I heard you say the name. Tansey."

"The same name."

"Your granny used to tell me all about her. About

how she'd died, and the little bits about her mother that she could remember. Because your granny was only three when it happened."

"That must have been, like, sad for you too," said Mary.

They were in the car again, heading for the hospital. The Sacred Heart.

"Yes, it was," said Scarlett. "But not really."

Her mother's !!!s were gone again, but Mary decided not to mention it. They were talking about death. But the strange thing was, Mary was enjoying the conversation.

"She never kept it secret," said Scarlett. "She never decided that it was too sad for me to hear about. And her own granny was lovely."

"My great-great-grandmother," said Mary.

"Oh gosh, I've lost count!" said Scarlett. "But, yes, I think so. She became the mammy."

"Not really," said Mary.

"No," her mother agreed. "You're right. But at least she had people who loved her."

She wiped her eyes.

So did Mary.

They smiled.

"What about your granddad?" Mary asked.

"Jim?" said Scarlett. "I remember Jim. He lived to be a ripe old age!"

"What does that mean?"

"You know what it means, Mary!"

"Yeah," said Mary. "But why 'ripe'? Why do people

say that? It's disgusting. It makes him sound like a rotten banana, or something that burst in my school bag and, like, ruined all my books and copies."

"What an image!" said Scarlett. "You're going to be a writer!"

"No, I'm not," said Mary. "It was just, like, a way of telling you that my banana burst in my bag and most of the books are covered in yeuk."

"Really?!"

"Really."

"We'll deal with it when we get back."

"Okay," said Mary.

Her plan had worked. It had only become a plan when she'd remembered what had happened to her school bag – *in* her school bag – while they were talking about her mother's granny, the other Tansey, less than a minute before. But the timing was perfect. She'd dreaded having to tell her mother. But now it was done and her mother would do most of the cleaning – Mary knew this; she could already see it – and they'd even have hot chocolate together when the job was done and they'd watch a film that only girls and women liked.

They were driving into the hospital car park. Scarlett stopped at the barrier and leaned out to grab a ticket from the machine.

"I'm always afraid I'll fall out of the car whenever I do that!" she said, and she laughed.

"At least it's the hospital car park," said Mary. "That's handy."

Scarlett laughed again.

"Oh dear," she said. "I hate this place."

"Me too," said Mary. "I'll tell her."

"Tell who?"

"Tansey."

"Tell her what?"

"That my great-granny had the same name as her. She's really nice."

Scarlett found a space on the second level, and she parked the car.

They were getting out, shutting their doors.

"I'd like to meet her," said Scarlett.

"Well, she's always out there," said Mary. "When I'm coming home."

"Maybe I'll come out tomorrow and say hello," said Scarlett.

"Okay," said Mary.

They walked out of the car park and along the path, through the people in dressing gowns who were smoking outside the front doors of the hospital, and into the place itself, past the shop that sold sweets and flowers that made Mary sneeze nearly every time she passed it, and down the long corridor that was full of people's whispers and the squeaks of their shoes and slippers. And into the empty lift that was wide enough for a car but was actually that size so that trolleys with people lying on them could fit into it, on their way to and from the operating theatres. Mary always expected to see a trolley with the sheet pulled over the person's face.

"Why do they put the sheet over the face?" she

asked her mother now, as the lift went up so slowly they weren't even sure it was moving.

"When someone's dead, do you mean?"

"Yeah," said Mary. "Obviously."

"Don't be rude."

"I'm not being rude," said Mary. "It never happens any other time."

"I don't know," said Scarlett. "What about very shy people?"

"What about them?"

"I'm sure they want the sheet over their faces when they're being trolleyed around."

"That's a joke, is it?" Mary asked.

"Yes, it is," said Scarlett.

"It's quite good," said Mary. "But I don't think this is either the time or the place for joking."

Scarlett laughed.

"You're impossible," she said.

"If I'm impossible," said Mary, "then how come I'm here? In this very slow lift?"

Finally, it stopped. About two days later – actually five seconds – the doors slid slowly open and Mary and Scarlett got out.

They passed the nurse that Mary didn't like and the other one she did like.

"How is she?" Scarlett asked.

"She's grand," said the nice nurse.

Mary's granny was asleep.

They sat beside her bed. She didn't wake up. This hadn't happened before. Mary's granny had either been awake or had woken when they'd arrived to see her. But now she lay there. Her head looked tiny against the pillow.

Mary sat up on the bed but her granny stayed asleep.

"She looks happy," Scarlett whispered.

It was true – if they wanted it to be true. Her face was calm. Her wrinkles were the ones she'd had as far back as Mary could remember, the wrinkles that had always been part of her granny. The wrinkles that were like lights, or paths that lit up, whenever her granny laughed – which was often. Paths that led to her granny's eyes – *all the better to see you with, my dear*.

They sat for a while longer – twenty minutes – hoping she'd wake up. Scarlett held her mother's hand. Then Mary did. It frightened her a bit, just before she touched the hand – just in case the hand was cold. But it wasn't. It was warm, and Mary thought she felt her granny's fingers squeeze her own, just slightly.

"We'd better go," Scarlett whispered. "The boys will be home."

Mary nodded, but still they sat until Mary heard the scrape, the squeak of her mother's chair and her mother leaned down to the face in the pillow and kissed it.

Mary slid off the bed, then leaned against the bed and tried to do what her mother had just done. But she wasn't tall enough to reach her granny without climbing back up. So she got up on the bed and kissed her granny's cheek.

"Ah, now," said her granny, although her eyes didn't open. "I know that kiss."

"Granny?"

She didn't answer.

"Granny?"

No answer.

"We'd better go," said Scarlett.

"She spoke to me," said Mary.

"I know," said Scarlett. "It's lovely."

Mary kissed her granny again, on her dry cheek, and got down off the bed.

Then she remembered something.

She got back up on the bed.

"Granny?"

Her granny's eyes stayed closed. Mary looked at her granny's mouth, and saw it move slightly, letting out a pop of air. Mary decided: her granny was listening, even if she was asleep.

"Granny," she said – she leaned down near to her granny's ear. "Tansey says it'll all be grand."

She watched, to see if her granny had heard, some sort of sign that the words had gone in. The eyes stayed shut, but the lines beside them shifted, very slightly.

"It'll all be grand," Mary said again, and tried to sound like Tansey.

Then she slid off the bed, and stood up straight when she felt her feet touch the floor.

"What was that about?" her mother asked, as they waited again for the lift.

"A message," said Mary.

"A message?"
"Yeah," said Mary.
"A message from who?"
"Tansey."
"The old woman."
"No. The footballer."
"Don't be cheeky."
"Sorry," said Mary.
"The old woman."
"She isn't old," said Mary. "But, yes."
"Does Tansey know your granny?"
"Yes," said Mary. "I think so."

Emer remembered it all her life. The day her mammy stopped. She was only three when it happened. She knew that all her life too. Her grandmother told her, and her daddy and her aunts and uncle.

You were only three.

You were only three, God love you.

A brave girl you were, and you only a little thing.

She remembered the egg. Her own egg. She'd brought it into the kitchen, to show it to her grandmother. She remembered running into the dark of the kitchen. But she couldn't remember what she'd run in from. And that saddened her, because she'd been out there with her mammy – she was told that – and, try as hard as she could – and she did try, for years – she couldn't pull her memory back, back out to the yard where her mammy had been walking behind her. She ran into the kitchen, too excited – too happy – to slow down and, before she could properly see, the egg was out of her hands, and she heard it smack the stone floor. Just a little flat noise, like a cheek full of air being tapped, and she knew she'd lost the egg before she could see the proof of it. She was crying before she fully understood. She'd nothing now to show her grandmother. She'd killed the egg.

She waited to be picked up. She knew she would be. It was still dark in the kitchen – her eyes weren't ready yet – but she could see her grandmother, the shape of her, at the range, worrying the food. Her daddy used to say that, about the way her grandmother stood at the range while she cooked. *Worrying the food, she is.*

Emer remembered this. She remembered it like it was yesterday, or even today, like it was something that had just finished happening. She was waiting to be picked up. And hands did pick her up. Two hands, and arms, went around Emer, hands that came from behind her. Her mammy had come into the kitchen – Emer hadn't heard her. Now, she felt herself being lifted, lifted gently, and turned so that her face was at her mammy's shoulder, then a little higher and she was looking straight at her mammy.

"What's the matter with you, at all?"

She remembered her mammy's voice. Each word was like a white cloud going past her eyes.

"The hegg!" she'd shouted.

This, she didn't remember. The egg – "the hegg".

Her grandmother had told her about the "h" she used to put in front of the egg.

"Did you drop it?"

"I did!"

"Ah, sure."

"It's dead."

Her memory took over again. These were words she could still hear, hers and her mammy's.

"It's not dead, love. It's only smashed."

"I killed it."

"No."

"I did!"

She was so happy in her mammy's arms, up there in the air at her face. She'd have cried and complained forever, just to stay up there.

"No, no," said her mammy. "There's no life in an egg that isn't under its hen. And, sure, look it. We've a whole basket full of them. D'you want another one, do you?"

"No," said Emer.

"Suit yourself, so."

The egg didn't matter any more. Emer didn't care about the egg. She could see it now, on the stone floor. She had her mammy all to herself, for a while at least. Her little brother, James the Baby, was still asleep. *There isn't a peep out of him.* She loved James the Baby – *he's the dote* – but sometimes she felt like she was at a window looking in at all the people she loved but who didn't know she was there. They were all fussing around James the Baby in his cot. But now James the Baby was fast asleep.

"It was only a hegg," said Emer.

"It was," said her mammy. "A fine class of an egg, mind, but only an egg."

She carried Emer across to the fire and Granddad's chair. Granddad was dead and up in heaven – *these years* – but the chair was still his. Her grandmother never sat in it. And Emer knew, because she'd heard her mammy and daddy talk about it, that they hadn't been able to get married until after Granddad had died and the farm had become her daddy's. *He was a difficult man*. She'd heard that whispered. The farm was Daddy's but the big chair still belonged to Granddad. But, even so, her mammy sat down in it whenever she wanted and no one ever complained, and not a peep from Granddad – *up above*.

The fireplace was huge, the size of a room, and the big chair was right beside it, nearly in it. The bellows wheel was beside the chair, and poor Parnell was asleep beside the wheel. Emer loved turning the wheel, and the whirr of the belt, when she wanted to be busy. But not now. She wouldn't be fussing this time, trying to get down off her mammy's lap. She was where she wanted to be. And not a peep out of James the Baby, wrapped up in his cot. It was a smelly chair but the smells were good ones. There was a smell like her daddy's pipe tobacco and there was a smell of hay. Even the smell of the greyhounds was good because it was only a smell and the greyhounds didn't come with it. The smell was the nicest part of the greyhound. It was a nice fat smell, even though the greyhounds were skinny, so skinny they frightened Emer. They were like the shadows of the animal, not the animal itself, the ghosts of beasts long dead – ghosts with teeth and claws.

Emer didn't know if these were the exact thoughts that had played in her mind that day, when she sat with her mammy that last time, but they might have been, because they were the thoughts she often had in that corner of the kitchen. There was nothing like smells for remembering. All her life, a certain smell – when she lifted the lid off a pot, or she pushed a trowel into the earth, or she took a dried sheet off the hedge – the smell would bring memories and thoughts right behind it, and the thoughts were nearly always of her mammy.

She sat on her mammy's lap. Her mammy's chin was right above her head. She could feel it like a warm roof over her. Her mammy's fingers worked at the button of Emer's coat. The buttons were big and the holes were stiff. Emer shifted a bit, to let her mammy get the coat off her. She remembered that coat. It was green tweed with a red fleck in the green, and it used to belong to her cousin. (Years later, her own daughter wore it whenever they went down to the farm.) The coat was off, beside them on the floor, safe away from the ashes. And the lovely arms were around her again.

"My dote," said her mammy. "How are you now?"

"I'm grand," said Emer. "Close your eyes."

It was their game. Emer lifted herself a little bit and kissed her mammy's chin.

"Ah now," said her mammy. "I know that kiss."

She opened her eyes.

"It's Emer!"

Then it all changed.

It was like the fire was suddenly too warm. The heat came off her mammy like it was something dangerous. The arms around Emer went slack.

Emer knew there was something wrong. She turned – she tried to turn – until she was able to see her mammy's face. She nearly fell off – the hands and arms weren't minding her any more. She shifted and nudged, and got angry while she was doing it. Then she could see. Her mammy was sitting back. And her eyes were shut. Sweat, like water, was pouring from the top of her face.

"Mammy?" said Emer. "Why have you your eyes closed?"

She knew her mammy wasn't asleep.

There was another body over Emer, close to her. It was her grandmother. She was standing beside the chair. Emer was right under her.

She watched her grandmother put her hand on her mammy's forehead.

"Oh Lord, the flu," said her grandmother. "Up to the bed with you, Tansey, girl."

"I'll be grand," said her mammy.

"Don't fight it," said her grandmother. "Of course, you'll be grand."

The grandmother's hands were on her then, and Emer was being lifted. She loved her grandmother but she didn't want to leave her mother's lap. She knew – she remembered, she was certain – there was something wrong. Sudden things were often bad. She whimpered. She couldn't think of words to say. She didn't want to stop what her grandmother was doing. Something was wrong, and her grandmother would mend it.

Her grandmother put Emer on the floor.

"There now."

Then she took hold of one of her mammy's arms, and Emer watched her mammy rising out of the chair. She was like an old woman who hadn't been budged in a long time. It was shocking. She had to look carefully, to make sure that it was her mammy.

And it was. Same dress, same face. She was standing now, shivering like she was very cold. She looked now at Emer, and smiled.

"Lucky me," she said. "Granny's bringing me up to the bed."

Everything was fine.

"Can I come with you?" said Emer.

"Granny will need your help down here," said her mother. "Won't you, Granny?"

"Oh, I will," said her grandmother. "I'd be hopeless without Emer."

They walked – her mother was able to walk – to the stairs. The passage was narrow and steep. Emer stayed where she was. There wasn't room for her now in the passage.

Her mother went up the first two steps. Emer remembered, all her life; it was exactly two. She often sat on the second step. Her mother stopped, and turned, and smiled at Emer. Then she kept going.

"I want to meet her," said Scarlett.

"Who?"

"Your Tansey," said Scarlett.

They were driving home from the hospital. The traffic was bad; the car wasn't moving.

"Okay," said Mary. "If we ever get home, like."

"We will! I know a short cut!"

"This *is* the short cut."

"Oh gosh, you're right! Ah, well!"

"She mightn't be there by the time we get home," said Mary. "And I don't know which apartment she lives in, like."

"Tomorrow then," said Scarlett.

"Okay."

The car in front of them moved –

"At last!"

– two feet.

"Oh, poo!"

"Language, Mammy."

"Sorry!"

But they got home, eventually. It was dark and they found Mary's two brothers, Killer and Dommo, in the kitchen, staring at the fridge and starving to death.

"See, boys?!" said Scarlett.

She opened the fridge door, and closed it, and opened it again.

"That's how it works."

They didn't laugh. They knew sarcasm when they heard it; they didn't like it. Scarlett didn't like it either, especially when she heard it coming from herself.

"Sorry, lads," she said. "It's just, we were at the hospital to see Granny and she didn't open her eyes all the time we were there. So, it's hard."

They nodded.

"And it took ages to get home."

They nodded again. One of them spoke.

"It's okay."

Mary filled the big pot with water.

"See, boys? This is how the tap works."

"Mary," said her mother. "We don't like sarcasm."

"You mightn't like it," said Mary. "But I love it."

She put the pot on the hob and listened to the lovely, dangerous whoosh of the gas. She put the lid on the pot, so the water would boil faster.

Scarlett took a packet of pasta shells out of the

press – and stopped. Mary saw, and the boys saw: their mother was crying.

The boys stood up, off their stools. They stood there. Mary went between them.

"Excuse me."

And she hugged Scarlett.

"It's called a hug, boys," she said. "And it costs nothing, like."

Scarlett laughed, and the boys smiled – kind of. They all ate the pasta and the boys washed the dishes, then went back upstairs.

Mary was alone with Scarlett. Her father played indoor football on Tuesdays after work, so he always came home late, sweating and stiff and usually limping.

"Will we try?" said Scarlett.

Mary knew what she was talking about.

"Okay."

They went outside. It was raining, but not heavily, and they were soon in under the trees. It wasn't cold. The trees always seemed louder at night, the swaying of the branches, the leaves brushing against one another. It often seemed that the trees were full of people whispering – especially tonight.

They stood on the street. There was no sign of anyone. No one walking a dog, no one heading down to the pub, no one coming home late, no one going to the bus stop. It was even quieter than usual.

But they waited.

"We'll give it a few more minutes," said Scarlett.

She didn't know what she expected. She tried to make sense of what Mary had been telling her about Tansey.

Not so long ago, Mary's bedroom had been full of her imaginary friends and animals. Mary could see them all. There were queens and elephants and other girls, and things like teddy bears that everybody could see but only Mary could see *and* hear. Tansey might have been Mary's latest imaginary friend, maybe her last one – her last goodbye to her childhood. Tansey – a name Mary had heard her granny say, many times over the years. Mary had spent weekends at her granny's house; there'd always been old photographs and chat. Her granny was dying, so Mary had made Tansey up, to fill the lonely space.

But Scarlett didn't think so. There was something about Mary's voice when she spoke about this Tansey. It was different, less matter of fact. The imaginary friends had always been real to Mary, as real as the bed and the shelves in her bedroom, as real as the rest of her family. But there was something in her voice when she spoke about this Tansey: doubt. Mary wondered if she'd really met this old woman who was actually quite young. The doubt in Mary's voice made Scarlett almost certain that Tansey did exist.

She existed. But what was she?

"You're out looking for me."

They heard her before they saw her. She seemed to have come out from behind one of the trees, although they hadn't seen her do it.

Mary wasn't surprised.

"Hi, Tansey," she said.

"Hello, yourself," said the woman.

She was dressed the same, the old-fashioned dress, the big boots covered in shining mud.

She looked at Scarlett.

"I know you," she said.

"I know you too," said Scarlett.

She hated it, and she refused to remember a time when she hadn't. Travelling with her parents, going places – anywhere – just made her want to vomit. Really vomit – she could feel it in her throat.

She hated this.

"Are we there yet?" said her mother.

And her father laughed, again.

They were going to her mother's old house in Wexford. They did it every summer, for two weeks, and the day after Christmas, for a few days. For as long as Scarlett could remember. And she hated it.

She hated it now. She could tell – she could see it. Her parents were getting excited. Like kids. Her mother leaned over in her seat and kissed her father. He turned and took his eyes off the road, so she could kiss him on the mouth. It was disgusting, people like them – people that old, and married – kissing like that, like they *liked* each other, fancied each other.

She looked out the window but it was all the same. Fields and trees; the Wicklow Mountains, or something, on one side; nothing much on the other side.

Her father was going bald. And her mother, lanky Emer – she should have been ashamed of herself. A woman her age, doing that, kissing, whatever age she was – ancient; fifty-five, or something. Her mother had been over forty when she'd had Scarlett, five years older than Scarlett's father. That was disgusting too.

It was hot in the car, even with the windows open. Her father had lit another cigarette. Little specks of ash landed on Scarlett's arm. But she said nothing. She was hoping they'd forgotten she was there. They probably had, anyway, the way they'd kissed, right in front of her, their own daughter.

Her father was always more excited before they went. He'd be packing the car for days. He'd even put Bilko, their dog – Scarlett's dog – into the back of the car a whole day before they were due to leave – this was a few years ago. He said it had been an accident, that Bilko had sneaked in when he wasn't looking, and it didn't really matter, because Bilko couldn't drive. Scarlett refused to remember laughing; she was positive she hadn't.

Bilko had died, a few months ago. Old age, they said – the vet and her parents. He'd been older than Scarlett, who was fourteen. There was a shed in the back garden and Scarlett had found him behind the shed, lying down, with blood coming out of him. They'd made her go to school and when she got home Bilko was gone. He'd been put down.

"It couldn't wait," her mother had said.

"You made me go to school!"

"That was a mistake," said her mother. "But when the vet said poor Bilko was dying, I had to make the decision. Waiting would have been cruel. Scarlett, love, I'm really sorry."

"You did it on purpose!"

Her mother had grown up on the farm; death was nothing to her. Dead lambs, dead cattle, dead pups, sacks of dead kittens, dead crows – Scarlett had heard about them all. Her mother was crying now, but Scarlett didn't care. She got out of the kitchen, up to her room. She searched the floor for Bilko's hair.

They'd promised her another dog. She'd said she didn't want one, that it was disgusting to even think about replacing Bilko, as if he was a light bulb or something. She told them she'd never forgive them, she'd never let them forget. They'd killed her dog – *her* dog – without letting her say goodbye.

They were coming into a town. She thought it was Arklow – or some other dump.

Her father had never been on a farm until he met her mother. He'd told Scarlett this loads of times, because she'd asked him to tell her. She remembered that. How he went to the farm, nervous about meeting her mother's grandmother.

"She doesn't like the Dublin fellas at all," her mother had told him. "She thinks Dublin fellas are nearly English."

"That's just thick," he said. "What's wrong with being English."

"It's just the way she is," said Emer.

"Anyway, I'm not English."

"Ah, sure, I know that. She just doesn't like Dublin."

"But she let you move there."

"Oh, she knew where the jobs were," said Emer. "You don't have to like carrots, even though you know they're good for you."

"I do like carrots," said Gerry – Scarlett's future father. "They're alright."

"I'm only saying," said Emer – Scarlett's future mother.

This had happened in 1961, five years before Scarlett was born. They were on the train. Emer's brother was going to meet them at Enniscorthy station.

Now, fourteen years after Scarlett had been born – it was July 1980 – they were heading back to Wexford, in her dad's car. They were in Arklow now, going down its one crumby street, and the car was hardly moving. There was a tractor in front of them, crawling.

"How come every time I drive out of Dublin I get stuck behind a bloody tractor?"

No one answered.

"It's the same tractor as well," said her dad. "Waiting to ambush me."

"Poor Gerry."

"Poor bloody me."

They were embarrassing.

More ash was landing on her arm. She wished it hurt, so she could scream – because she really, really wanted to.

She remembered her dad telling her about that first time he went to Wexford.

"Right," he said – Scarlett was sitting in beside him, in his big chair. "Where was I? So, we got off the train in Istanbul—"

"Dad!"

"Okay. We got off the train in Enniscorthy."

"Which, by the way, has a lot more going for it than Istanbul," said her mother, who was sitting in her corner.

"Mammy!"

"Is there a strawberry fair in Istanbul, is there?"

"Mammy!"

"Or a Vinegar Hill?"

"Mammy!"

"Okay," said her dad. "We got off the train in Enniscorthy. It was dark."

"It was," said her mother. "It often is at night."

"Your Uncle Jim – James the Baby – was there, waiting. A nice fella."

"He is. A fine man. It's a mystery how he never found himself a woman."

"Mammy!"

Her father spoke over Scarlett's head, to her mother.

"It took you a fair while to find yourself a man, missis," he said.

"And what a man I found, God love me."

"Ahem," said Scarlett. "I'm here."

"Cheeky as ever."

Her dad looked down at her.

"So, anyway," he said. "We got into your uncle's old Ford."

"I sat in the front," said her mother. "Because I'm taller than your dad."

"And significantly older."

"So, I needed the leg room."

"So, anyway," said her dad. "I got into the back. Because, like your mother said, I'm a bit of a leprechaun."

"I said no – such – thing!"

"Well, actually, you did."

"When did I ever call you a leprechaun?"

"The first time we met."

"I didn't."

"You bloody well did."

"When did I say that?"

"At the match," said her father. "At Croker – Croke Park. Dublin against Wexford," he told Scarlett. "That's where I met your mother. And we won – Dublin did."

"You were lucky."

"I was standing on Hill 16 and I asked the tall woman standing in front of me to shift a bit, so I could watch the Dubs trounce the bog men, and she turned to me and said—"

"Don't listen to him."

"'Why?' she said," said Scarlett's father. "'Are you some class of a leprechaun?'"

"I said it before I knew what I was saying. It's too late to apologize, I suppose."

"Scarlett," said her dad. "Have you ever heard the sound of twenty-five thousand people laughing at you at the same time?"

"No."

"It's a horrible experience," he said.

"Still, though," said her mother. "You thought I was gorgeous."

"Well, that's true," he said. "I've always had a thing about giraffes."

"Can we get back to the story, please?" said Scarlett.

"So, anyway," said her dad. "I threw our cases – *I* carried the cases, mind you – I threw them into the boot of Jim's jalopy and got into the back seat, all set to go. And Jim was behind the wheel already. He started the engine and we were rolling. Then the car door right beside me opened. I nearly fell out, there were no seat belts in those days. And a greyhound climbed in on top of me. I swear to God. And your mother started to scream, because she hates greyhounds."

"God, I do. Hate them, hate them. Always hated them. Everything about them."

"And another one crawled in, after the first one. They were right on top of me. I wasn't sure if they were licking or biting me. Then something else was climbing in, and it was too fat to be a greyhound."

"Stop that, Gerry."

"It was Great-Granny," said Scarlett.

"That's right," said her dad. "It was your great-grandmother, in all her glory. With another bloody greyhound, and the cup one of them was after winning at the dog track. A big silver thing that she whacked against the side of my head when she was climbing in. Nearly knocked me out. I thought I was bleeding and the dogs would go mad with the smell of the blood. And your mother was still screaming. And your uncle, James the bloody Baby, was whistling 'Your Cheatin' Heart'."

"That was his favourite, alright."

"And the woman with the cup turns to me and says—"

"You're the fella from Dublin."

"That's right."

"And what did you say?" Scarlett asked, although she already knew the answer.

"I said, 'I think so.'"

"Why didn't you just say 'Yes'?"

"Because there was a greyhound trying to take the wallet out of my inside pocket and another one chewing my tie and Emer's granny was more or less parked up on my lap and there was another dog whispering into my ear and your mother was still screaming so, well, I was a bit confused."

He stretched his legs. "But it was grand," he said. "We were all pals by the time we got to the farm."

"You're not nearly a leprechaun, Dad," said Scarlett.

"Oh, I know that," he said. "But, let's face it, your mother is a bit of a giraffe."

Scarlett looked at the giraffe now, her mother, lanky Emer. They were out of Arklow. Gorey was next, she thought, and another crawl up a long, nothing street. Her mother was sitting up, leaning forward, like she was pushing the car, trying to get there sooner. To the house where she'd grown up, the house with the straw roof where her granny had reared her because her mother had died of the flu. Her name was Tansey. Scarlett knew all about it. Tansey had walked into the house just after feeding the greyhound and she picked up little Emer because she was crying, because she'd dropped an egg, and they sat down in the big chair. And everything started to change – the certainties of her mother's life vanished, right in front of her eyes. She watched her mother going up the stairs, and it was the last time she saw her. Scarlett knew all about it.

"I want a greyhound," said Scarlett.

"You're my grandmother," said Scarlett.

And the woman, Tansey, nodded.

Yes.

Mary should have been scared. Her mother's grandmother was dead. She'd died years ago, long before her mother had been born. She'd died when Mary's granny, her mother's mother, had been a little girl. She knew all this.

But Mary wasn't scared. The way her mother and Tansey were looking at each other, she thought – she knew – there was no need to be scared. At all.

But she was curious.

"How does that work?" she said.

Scarlett jumped.

"God!"

"Sorry," said Mary.

"No, no!" said Scarlett. "It's just a bit of a shock!" She laughed. "A nice one!"

"You hope," said Mary.

"Yes," said Scarlett. "Of course! Sorry, Mary, what was it you wanted to know?"

"Well," said Mary. "How does it work, like? How can Tansey be your granny?"

"Can you guess?" said Tansey.

"Guessing isn't fair," said Mary. "Just tell me."

"Well," said Tansey. "I'm a ghost. It sounds a bit daft, but I'm the ghost of your great-granny."

She looked at Mary. "Are you surprised?" she asked.

"Not really," said Mary. "If you *are* my great-granny, then you have to be a ghost or something, like. Because she – *you've* been dead for ages."

"Clever girl," said Tansey.

"Prove it," said Mary.

"Prove that you're a clever girl?"

"No," said Mary. "Prove you're a ghost."

"Alright, so," said Tansey. "Just a little thing. Look now."

Mary and Scarlett watched Tansey disappear. They watched as she faded, and became see-through. They could see the tree trunk behind her – through her. She was nearly gone. But, just when Mary began to think they'd never see Tansey again and she started to feel a bit frightened, the fading stopped. The colour came back, and the hair and the eyes and the features of her face – Tansey coughed, and became a solid woman again.

"That was cool," said Mary.

"What does that mean?" said Tansey.

"What does what mean?"

"Cool."

"She means great," said Scarlett. "Or impressive."

"Oh then, grand," said Tansey. "The fading bit is easy enough, but coming back can be a bit tricky."

"Is that why you coughed?"

"That's the reason," said Tansey. "It feels like my lungs are filling up with air. As if I'm alive, you know. It's always a bit of a shock."

Tansey turned to Scarlett.

"You look nice," she said.

"She is nice," said Mary. "Kind of."

The two women with her smiled and, now – suddenly – Mary felt scared. She stepped back, and nearly tripped on the root of a tree that had broken through the concrete path. She steadied herself, and looked again.

"What's wrong?" said Scarlett.

Mary said nothing.

"What's wrong?"

Mary looked from one woman, to the other. She felt as if she was going to cry.

It made no sense.

"Mary?" said Scarlett. "What's the matter?"

"You look the same."

Scarlett smiled.

"Well," she said. "That's what I was always told!

That I looked just like my grandmother!" She turned to Tansey. "Like you—"

She stopped smiling, and she understood why Mary was worried.

"You look *exactly* the same," said Mary.

"Yes."

"And what's wrong with that?" Tansey asked. "Sure, wasn't I a ringer for my own mother? God be good to her."

"Change yourself," said Mary.

"Mary, don't be rude," said Scarlett.

"I'm not being rude," said Mary. "She's too like you, Mammy. I'll mix you up."

Then a thought hit her. "That's what she wants."

"What do you mean?" said Scarlett.

Mary grabbed Scarlett's arm. "Come on, I want to go home."

It was important – vital. Mary had to separate them, get her mother home as quickly as possible.

"Wait," said Tansey. "Wait."

There was no sound from anywhere, not even a car far down the street, or someone's shoe on the footpath at the corner; or a distant siren, a police car or an ambulance. There were just the leaves above them, whispering, and the branches groaning. For the first time, Mary knew what a frightening street she lived on – if she let it, or if she wanted it to be.

But she didn't want it to be frightening. So she didn't run. And she let go of her mother's arm.

She looked from Tansey, back to Scarlett. They

were still exactly the same. Even their dresses, the old-fashioned dresses, looked as if they came from the same shop. Only the boots were different. If Mary had just arrived, it would have been the only thing she could have been sure about: one of them wore red boots that belonged to her mother. But it wasn't necessarily her mother who wore them.

"Mammy?"

Only one woman spoke.

"Yes?"

The woman with the red boots.

That calmed Mary.

There were other little differences – she could see that now. The wind shifted a branch above them and the street light lit the two women. The dresses weren't the same at all. Her mother's was newer, less faded, with zips. Her hair was darker – her mother's colour. The little black freckle just beside her mouth was exactly where it should have been. She was definitely looking at her mother. Tansey – the ghost – was different enough now, and herself.

"It's weird," said Mary.

"What's weird, Mary?" her mother asked, gently.

"You look older than her," said Mary.

Scarlett looked at Tansey.

"That *is* weird," she agreed.

"I can't help that," said Tansey. "I was only a young woman when I died."

"But it was years ago."

"I don't think that matters," says Tansey.

"You don't, like, know for certain?"

"Ah sure," said Tansey. "Who knows anything for certain?"

"It just doesn't seem fair," said Scarlett. "You're sixty years older than me but you look gorgeous."

"I'll be honest with you, girl," said Tansey. "Give me the wrinkles and the sore teeth any day. I loved my life when I lost it."

"I wasn't being serious," said Scarlett.

"I know that," said Tansey. "But I was."

She smiled – Mary thought she did.

"As serious as death," said Tansey. "Just so you know."

Mary had gone from terrified to sad, without really noticing.

"You said I was your grandmother," Tansey said to Scarlett. "But, you know, I'm not. The blessed flu took hold of me just when I was only starting to be a mother."

"*The blessed flu*," said Mary. "You sound like a grandmother."

"That's a lovely thing to say," said Tansey.

She said nothing for a while. Then she looked at Scarlett.

"Your mother was only a little thing when I died," she said.

She turned to Mary. "Even younger than you."

"I know," said Mary. "Much younger."

"And I always wondered," said Tansey, "while I still had my health, what it would be like to watch my daughter grow and become a mother."

She smiled again.

"D'you know what?" she said. "You're the ringer for your granny."

"How can I be?" said Mary. "I'm only twelve."

"Your granny was a girl too once," said Tansey.

"I'm cold," said Mary.

"Ah now," said Tansey. "You sound like her too."

"Okay," said Mary. "But listen. This has to stop."

"What has to stop?"

"This you're-like-your-granny stuff," said Mary. "You're like your granny, you sound like your granddad, your cat barks like your granny's dog."

"Mary!"

"You're cheeky like her too," said Tansey. "But fair enough. No young one wants to be told she looks like an old one."

"That's not it," said Mary. "This is stupid. I'm cold. I'm going in."

"Mary!"

"I'm not being cheeky," Mary told Scarlett. "I'm *not*. It *is* stupid. You look like your granny and I look like mine. So what, like? Your granny is a ghost and mine is dying. And that's the only thing that isn't stupid."

Scarlett spoke quietly. The branches above grabbed at her words.

"What do you mean, Mary?"

Mary pointed at Tansey. "Why is she here? Why is she here now?"

She turned to Tansey. "What do you want?"

"I want to speak to Emer," she said. "I need to speak to her."

"Why now?" said Mary.

She didn't know why she was talking like this. It was as if she was listening to someone else – the woman she was going to be in the future.

It annoyed her, and impressed and frightened her – and reassured her. Because she knew she was right. Her world was suddenly full of the dead and the dying, people she loved and people she was supposed to love – and people she didn't know, even if they did look like the people she knew she loved. She needed to know. There was a dead woman two steps away from her, shimmering at the edge of Mary's life. She was the mother of her granny – she was supposed to be.

Tansey hadn't answered.

"Why now?" Mary asked again. "Have you spoken to her before, since you died?"

"No, I haven't," said Tansey. "I let her be."

"So, why *now*?" said Mary.

"She needs me now," said Tansey.

She lay on the bed. Her eyes were closed. She was asleep.

But she wasn't.

She was afraid to sleep. She wasn't sure what sleep was any more. The luxury and the need were gone out of it, and the warm, reassuring fact that she'd wake up when it was over.

There'd been times when she was asleep, lots of times, since she was a girl, when she'd wake suddenly, her head would jump on the pillow, because she'd fallen in her dream – out of her dream – off a cliff, off a roof – a sudden fall, and horrible. But she'd wake, and stay awake for a while, and it would be grand. She'd know where she was. The wall was where it should be, and the window. And, later, her husband,

Gerry, would be lying on his side of the bed, even – it seemed – years after he died. She'd feel him there and the terror would disperse before she had time to think of it.

The terror now was that she'd fall but wouldn't wake. She'd keep falling, and the fall would never stop.

She wasn't tired. She couldn't really remember what tiredness felt like, or the glory of a good ol' stretch and yawn. *There's enough of you to stretch, God knows.* She wasn't sure why she was so afraid. She liked her life, even without Gerry – once his absence became bearable and the memories could be sweet. But she knew, she'd always known, there'd be an end. She'd seen her mother die. She'd been sitting on her lap when that started, when death pounced and took her.

Up the stairs.

A few days later, they brought her up, to say goodbye. *Where's Mammy going?* She didn't hear the answers. *Why is she going?* They brought her up the stairs. She remembered holding her grandmother's big rough hand. She remembered her father was around, talking to men outside. She remembered James the Baby crying, and more people in the kitchen than usual. Women. Millions of them. She didn't know any of them until they bent down to her. Her Auntie Ellen, her Aunt Maud. And women she saw on Sundays only, outside the church. Other women she'd never seen before. They made tea. They made sandwiches. She heard more women whispering, praying, somewhere else. And men too, smoking, talking quietly, drinking bottles of porter and little glasses of whiskey, going outside into the cold, coming back in, chatting softly about the greyhounds and their farms.

She hadn't seen her mammy since the stairs.

She'd heard a cough.

She'd heard feet, rushing.

She'd heard silence. Absolute silence.

Her grandmother held her hand. The bedroom door was open, at the top of the stairs. The curtains were closed. There were women in there, kneeling at the bed, praying, whispering to themselves. Emer could see their rosary beads. She saw one line of beads move as fingers finished with one bead and moved on to the next one.

The women heard her grandmother's weight on the floorboards, and they stood up. One of them smiled at Emer. Emer knew her, and she'd see her many times, later on, when she went to school and sat beside the woman's daughter, Noreen Cash, and Noreen became Emer's best friend, until the whole family of Cashes, every one of them, went to America, when Emer and Noreen were ten.

The women stood back.

And Emer saw her mammy.

"Why are there pennies on her eyes?"

"To help her on her way."

"Where's she going?"

"Up to heaven, that's where she's going."

"Am I going as well?"

"No, girl. Not yet."

She watched, for her mammy to move. To take the pennies from off her eyes.

"I want to go to heaven."

"Oh, you will. Don't worry. We're all on our way."

"I want to go now. With Mammy."

Her mammy's face was lovely there, except for the pennies. Her hair was combed and shining, even in the dark. Her hands were together, on top of the quilt. Her rings were perfect and polished.

"I'm cold," said Emer.

"It's cold, right enough," said her grandmother. "Say goodbye to your mammy."

Emer looked at her mother.

"She's not asleep."

"She's not."

Her grandmother picked her up. She held Emer over the bed, as if she was going to drop her on to her mammy and her mammy would wake and laugh and catch her.

"Kiss her goodbye and we'll go on down to the fire."

"No!"

She remembered that *No!* She could still hear it, more than eighty years later. It had followed her everywhere, all her life.

"No!"

She remembered – years later it was – and she stood beside Gerry at the altar. When Father O'Casey said, "Do you, Emer Mary Stafford, take this man to be your lawfully wedded husband?", she'd said "Yes!", like that, and she'd started laughing. And everyone in the church joined in, happy to see Emer so happy.

That was what she'd done, all her life. She'd tried to even the score, by saying Yes so often that the No would fade to nothing. But it never had. And, after a while, she was glad it hadn't. It was only a word and it was a line right back to her mother.

"No!"

Her mother wouldn't have minded. She'd have understood. The little girl was terrified, and why wouldn't she have been? Brown pennies over her mammy's eyes, and a perishing cold that seemed to come off her mammy in the middle of the bed.

Still.

She wished she could have gone back. She'd have let herself be lowered, right down to her mammy's face and lips. She'd have kissed her.

Emer lay there now. She could hear the hospital business, the usual stuff – nurses' shoes squeaking, trolley wheels squeaking. Everything squeaked in a hospital.

Her daughter had kissed her. Her granddaughter had kissed her. *Ah now, I know that kiss*. She'd been kissed by people who loved her. But still. She'd been kissed and that was lovely, but she didn't want to go. She'd always loved breathing, especially on the cold days, grabbing the air, letting it go, being able to see it. She couldn't breathe deep any more, and she hadn't run for the bus in more than thirty years. Although – she remembered – she'd caught that bus. And even the aches and pains that had joined her as she got older – she'd liked them. They were reminders – the back, the knee, the achy wrists – they were even friends: *Feel that now, Emer. You're alive.*

Emer lay there.

I'm alive.

I'm lanky Emer.

I'm long, tall Emer.

I'm a few inches shorter but I'm alive.

"I'm alive."

They sat in the kitchen.

"Do ghosts drink tea?"

"They don't," said Tansey. "But this ghost would love to see a cup of tea in front of her. It'd be lovely."

Mary watched as Tansey looked up at the light. There was no light shade over the bulb. Scarlett had taken it down once, to wash it, but it had never gone back up. It was on top of the fridge, with a lot of other stuff that was waiting to be put somewhere else. Tansey was staring straight up at the bulb but she didn't squint.

"That electric light is fierce," she said. "We didn't have it in my day."

"They didn't have it when I was a girl either," said Scarlett.

"Did they not have the electric in Dublin?" said Tansey. "I thought they had all that kind of thing."

"No," said Scarlett. "I meant, on the farm."

"Oh," said Tansey. "It's powerful stuff but, still and all, it might be a good idea to turn it off. It's hard for me to stay looking solid under that bright light. I'd say it must be shining right through me."

It was – or it seemed to be. It wasn't frightening any more, but Tansey definitely looked less alive in the house than she had outside. Her dress, under the light, looked like it had been washed far too many times. Tansey looked like a film of herself, projected on to a screen in a room that wasn't dark enough; the sound was fine but the picture was cloudy and annoying.

"Anyone walking in on us," said Tansey, "might get a bit of a fright. And we wouldn't want that."

"Yes, we would," said Mary. "But okay."

She turned off the light. "There."

"Thank you."

Mary sat again, and looked across at Tansey.

Tansey couldn't drink tea, and she couldn't taste or smell. But she could see and she could tell when lights were too bright, although the brightness itself didn't seem to bother her. Mary didn't think Tansey could feel rain, or the cold. But she *was* cold. Mary could feel it coming from her. It was as if the cold was pulling at Tansey, breaking her up, trying to take her away from them, back somewhere. But that was weird too – *weirder* – because she looked quite relaxed.

Scarlett stood beside the kettle, waiting for it to start humming, so she'd have something to do, put the tea bags into cups, put the sugar on to the table – anything. The strangeness was catching up on her. She'd have started to shake if she'd let herself. There was a ghost in the kitchen, and she was supposed to behave as if it was normal. She knew, although she wasn't sure how, that something important was going to happen, something to do with her mother.

They heard a thump from upstairs, something or someone falling.

"The boys," Scarlett explained. "My sons."

"Making the racket that only boys can make," said Tansey.

"That's right," said Scarlett, and she smiled.

"Will I get to meet them?" Tansey asked.

"I think so," said Scarlett.

She nodded at the fridge.

"That's what will get them to come down," she said.

"What's that when it's at home?" said Tansey.

"It's a fridge, like," said Mary, and she laughed – it was so silly.

"Like a meat safe," said Scarlett. "Refrigerator's the full word."

"Keeps everything fresh," said Mary.

"Is there room in there for me?" said Tansey.

They laughed before they thought too much about it.

"Nearly ready here," said Scarlett.

Tansey looked at Mary's big eyes looking back at her. She could tell: Mary wanted to ask her a question.

"Ask away," said Tansey. "Ask away."

"Well," said Mary. "Like. Why are there ghosts?"

"Do you mean," said Tansey, "why do I exist?"

"Yeah," said Mary.

"That sounds a bit rude, Mary," said Scarlett.

"It's fine," said Tansey. "It's not even a bit rude."

"Oh, good!" said Scarlett. "Because I wanted to ask it as well!"

"Well," said Tansey. "Here goes. Mind you, before I start—"

"Yes?"

"I can only speak for myself," said Tansey.

"That's better than nothing," said Mary.

"It is," Tansey agreed. "It is. So. Well. People die. But sometimes – quite often – they aren't ready to leave. There are things they'd be worried about."

"Like their children?" said Mary.

"With me," said Tansey, "it was certainly the children. And probably with most other ghosts. They don't go away, after the funeral. They linger. To make sure that everything is grand and the people they love are getting on with their lives. They hang around."

"For how long?" asked Mary.

"That depends," said Tansey. "But that's what happened me. I was disturbed when the last breath came. There was no peace in it. I was too worried – not just sad – about Emer and little James."

"James the Baby," said Mary.

Tansey smiled.

"That was what we called him," she said. "Where did you hear that, tell me?"

"Granny told me," said Mary.

"Of course she did," said Tansey.

"So," said Mary. "Did you not really die?"

"Oh, I died alright," said Tansey. "Oh God, I did. But—"

They heard a rumbling noise from above that came quickly nearer, and the boys charged into the kitchen, in a race to the fridge that Killer was winning.

They stopped when they saw Tansey.

"We're talking about death, boys!" said Scarlett.

"Cool," said Dommo.

"These are the famous boys, are they?" said Tansey.

"That's right!" said Scarlett. "Dominic and Kevin! Boys, this is Tansey, your – well – neighbour!"

"Hi."

"Hi."

They were gone, back out, before they'd even made it to the fridge. Mary listened to the noise going back up the stairs.

"Too many women in the room," said Tansey. "They couldn't cope."

"You're probably right!"

"Oh, I am," said Tansey. "I didn't even have to be a ghost. Was my James like those two lads?"

"My mother says he was a scamp!" said Scarlett.

"Oh good," said Tansey.

"But were you not watching?" Mary asked. "Like now?"

"I'll get to that," said Tansey. "But I have to get there first."

She sat up, as if remembering she had a story to tell.

The kettle had boiled and turned itself off, and Scarlett poured the water into the cups. Tansey watched. Mary could tell; Tansey wanted to ask questions about the electric kettle, the tea bags, the things she hadn't known when she was alive. Mary wondered again: what had Tansey been doing all the years since she'd died?

It was if Tansey heard Mary's thoughts.

"I was never too worried about James the Baby," she said. "He was only a baby, still new. It was sad, alright, but he'd be grand. He wouldn't miss me, just maybe the idea of me. He'd see a mammy in a book and he'd wonder about that. It would break your heart thinking about it, but I don't think heartbreak is strong enough to make a ghost out of you. Because it's your own heartbreak and it can die with the rest of you. So, it wasn't James the Baby that held me back. I knew he'd have Jim and Jim's mother."

She looked straight at Mary.

"But Emer," she said. "Your granny. That was different. Emer, I fretted about. I lived longer than should have been possible. Did they ever tell you that?" she asked Scarlett.

"Yes," said Scarlett. "They said you fought it and kept asking for Emer."

"I'm glad of that," said Tansey. "I needed Emer to know that, after I'd gone. That I tried my best. I'm glad now she knew. I'd cry if I could, girls."

She smiled.

"So," she said. "It was Emer made a ghost of me. She wouldn't let me go. I had to make sure she'd be grand."

"She was grand!" said Scarlett.

"But I was never sure," said Tansey.

Scarlett put a cup in front of Tansey.

"Oh, look now."

And one in front of Mary. Then she sat down.

"So," said Tansey. "I lingered."

"No one ever mentioned a ghost," said Scarlett. "Or even – sorry – a cold spot in the house, you might have—"

"No, no," said Tansey. "I stayed clear of the house. I'd no wish to disturb the peace or mending. But I had to stay near, all the same."

She looked down at her tea.

"I was never that mad about tea at all," she said. "You know, the way others go daft if they don't have a cup every hour. I was never like that. But now—"

She smiled again – there was nothing sad in her smile. "I'd love to taste this tea."

"It must be hard being a ghost," said Mary.

"Well, it is," said Tansey. "It's harder than living. Especially if you die young, like I did. I hope now I'm not depressing you two ladies."

"No!"

"No way."

"I felt terrible guilty, you see. I couldn't help it and I still can't. Because I died too soon and I died too quickly. I know it wasn't my fault but, even when you're dead, you can't help your feelings. So. Drink your tea there. I'm grand, don't be staring at me."

Mary and Scarlett did what they were told. The tea was much too hot for Mary, but she said nothing. She sipped and scalded herself, and knew she was doing the right thing, being calm in front of Tansey.

"So," said Tansey. "Like I said, I felt guilty and very unsettled. I'd left things unfinished, not properly looked after. I suppose now all mothers would feel that way if they were leaving little ones behind."

"And fathers," said Mary.

"Fair enough," said Tansey. "You're right, you're right. But the saddest ghosts, I'd say – male or female – would be the ones who died when their children were still children, in school maybe, just starting to grow up. The poor ghosts feel terrible about it. So, they stay. They linger. D'you know, I hate that word, linger. It's too cosy, altogether. They stay to see if everything is alright. To see their children grow up, for a while. To make sure the children are fine."

"Is that what happened you?" Mary asked Tansey.

"That's exactly what," said Tansey. "I couldn't leave Emer."

"Why did you stay so long?"

"Oh Lord," said Tansey. "That's the question."

Scarlett was five when she found her mother crying in the milking parlour. It was the second day of their summer holiday. The rain had stopped during the night, when they were all asleep. Scarlett slept in a room high up in the house, right under the straw, and she could hear the mice up there, but they didn't frighten her at all. She thought mice were lovely.

She put on her holiday clothes, her old holey jeans and her plastic sandals, and she went carefully down the wooden steps, from her little room to the landing, and then down the dark stairs to the kitchen. The smell of rashers got stronger as she went down each step. But she didn't rush. She went slowly, carefully. She couldn't really see in front of her, until she turned the corner in the stairs and the light from the open kitchen door came in a hard, straight line across the floor to where the stairs started, and she was safe.

The kitchen was empty. That meant she was the last one up this morning. She listened, and she knew: the whole house was empty. It was so bright and warm in the kitchen, she knew it was quite late. She'd had a great sleep. But now she wanted to be awake. And she couldn't be really awake unless there were people to see her and hear her.

She went out into the yard.

She could hear a tractor far away. She knew that was her Uncle James the Baby. She guessed that her daddy had walked down the lane to the shop, to get his paper and his cigarettes. So that just left her mammy, somewhere. Scarlett didn't call out yet. She wanted to surprise her.

She went to the gate of the kitchen garden. A piece of wire held it closed. It was easy to lift, even though she didn't have to go in. She could see that the garden was empty, just rows of lettuces and other vegetables, some of them with huge fat leaves that looked like shoulders, bent over, protecting their little baby vegetables. She didn't like the strawberry plants, or the way they didn't grow up; they were sneaky. She stayed looking into the garden for a while longer, just to make sure her mammy wasn't behind one of the apple trees or at the very back of the garden, at the gooseberry bushes, where – her mammy told her – people went to wee, before the house had a toilet. She waited a little while more, but there was no one down there.

She could still hear the tractor, and she could hear the crows giving out, in the big trees behind the kitchen garden.

Next, Scarlett went to the shed that was full of nothing except a smell. The smell was so bad, it made her daddy laugh and cough whenever he stuck his head into it. Scarlett knew her mammy wouldn't be there, but she looked in anyway, into the dark and the stink.

"Hello?"

Nothing answered.

All the sheds were whitewashed and the walls were uneven, as if big flat hands behind the whitewash kept pushing them out of place. Uncle James the Baby whitewashed them every couple of years but the inside walls of the empty shed were covered in green stuff that seemed to climb up from under the ground. There was no door any more, just two big rusty hinges where the door had hung. It was cold in there, and not nice. But Scarlett loved looking into it, from a safe distance. She'd wondered why it was the only shed that wasn't used. The rest of the farmyard was bright and useful. She'd asked her Uncle James the Baby about it, the night before.

"What shed would we be talking about now?"

"The one with the smell," said Scarlett.

"That'll be the pigs," said Uncle James the Baby, as he took off his boots at the kitchen door.

"There are no pigs," said Scarlett.

"But the smell lingers long after they leave," said Uncle James the Baby. "Oh God, it does linger."

"Why did the pigs leave?"

"I told them to," said Uncle James the Baby. "'Off with you, pigs,' I said. 'My niece is coming to stay and she'll be wanting your room to sleep in.'"

"Yeuk!"

Uncle James the Baby came into the kitchen. He was high up, like Scarlett's mammy. He had to bend at the kitchen door and his hair stood up on top of his head after he took his cap off, and it made him look even higher. He sat down in the big chair that used to belong to his granddad and now belonged to his dad, although his dad, Jim – Scarlett's granddad – was in the hospital in Wexford with something wrong with his stomach. They were going to see him tomorrow. They'd be bringing him grapes and *Ireland's Own*, his favourite magazine. She watched Uncle James the Baby lower himself into the chair. He had to fold himself – that was how it looked – like her dad's penknife, and it seemed to take forever before he was sitting properly in the chair.

"Myself and your granddad," he said, "we decided we didn't want the pigs any more and we'd concentrate on the cows. It must be ten years ago now. So, the pigs went off to sausage land, but the smell stayed behind. They don't put the smell into the sausages, thank God. But we're stuck with it. Did you see the trough in there, did you?"

"What's a trough?"

"It's – it'd be like the bucket for their food. Made of stone. There's a water trough down in the village, where the horses drank their water in the days of the horses. D'you know it, do you?"

"Yes. Dad always sits there and reads the front of his paper."

"That's right," said Uncle James the Baby. "Well, that's a trough."

Scarlett stood at the shed door now and looked at the trough she hadn't noticed before. It was lower than the one in the village, because, she knew, the pigs' legs were shorter, so the trough had to be nearer the ground. It was much longer than the trough in the village. It went down the side of the shed, all the way. That was where the pigs had had their food, in the olden days. She wanted to see if there was any old food still in the trough. But she didn't go in.

She crossed the yard to the greyhounds. The tractor was still going, and she guessed that her daddy was down in the village by now, sitting on the side of the trough – she knew what a trough was now – reading his paper and having a cigarette.

She stood at the fence.

Her mammy didn't like the greyhounds. They were too skinny, she said, and too needy – although Scarlett didn't know what that meant.

Scarlett didn't mind them. They were big and skinny, alright – there were four of them – but they were shiny and they reminded her of the seals she'd seen at the zoo when they'd gone there for her birthday. Their backs were like the seals' backs, when they ran. They all came up to the fence to see her, but they didn't go mad or anything. She knew her mammy definitely wasn't in there with the greyhounds, so she turned away.

"Bye bye," she said.

And she went back across the yard to the milking parlour. She went carefully around the old dried-up cow poo, and the poo from this morning that was nearer the door and hadn't dried up yet. There were diseases and little, nearly invisible things in cow poo.

She loved the milking parlour. She always loved the way the cows came slowly up the lane, by themselves, as if they were on their way to school. Her dad once said that they should have had school bags on their backs, and caps with holes for their horns. Then the cows all turned, sometimes pushing each other – but not hard, like they were forming a queue – and went into the parlour, straight to their places in the parlour, to be milked. They all had their place and they all knew where they had to stand. Sometimes, at home, she dreamed about the cows walking up the lane, a line of them that never ended until she woke up. Once, in the dream, there was a television on the other side of the lane but Scarlett couldn't see what was on, because the cows kept walking past it. She didn't get annoyed or try to move. She was happy looking at the cows. They were so close, she could rub them.

This wasn't a cow time, though. She'd missed the one early this morning, because she'd been asleep, and it was ages before the next one, just before the humans had their tea – after the cows were put back in their field and Uncle James the Baby had washed his hands all the way up to his elbows.

The parlour was quiet now but not a bit scary. There was water on the floor where Uncle James had used the hose after he'd finished with the cows that morning. The parlour was always nice and cool when the day outside was getting hot, and there was none of the green stuff growing on the walls. The shiny steel machines were all hanging in their places. "I don't know myself with the electric," Scarlett had heard Uncle James the Baby tell her parents. Scarlett didn't know what he'd meant, exactly, but she thought it had something to do with the machine things that went over the cows' milk things and milked the cows for him while he could lean against the wall and chat. Before he had the machines, he'd had to do it all himself, with a man from up the lane called Lefty, who had gone off to England to work in a factory.

She stepped into the parlour. She didn't have to be careful now because the concrete floor had been washed and it was grand and clean. She walked right in and heard her mammy. Then she saw her. She knew it was her mammy, before she could see. Her mammy wasn't hiding, or anything. She was standing close to the wall, just behind where Scarlett now stood, and her forehead was leaning against the whitewash. She wasn't bawling, just crying quietly. Weeping.

"Mammy?"

Her mammy was so tall, Scarlett couldn't see her face clearly, because the sunlight from outside brightened the ground and some of the wall but not all the high parts of the parlour.

Scarlett saw her mammy wipe her face with the sleeve of her cardigan. Her mammy usually had a handkerchief up the sleeve, but she mustn't have had one there this morning.

Scarlett saw her bend down a little and smile.

"What?"

"Are you crying?"

"I am."

"Why are you crying?"

"I'm sad," said Scarlett's mammy. "I'm a bit sad. Or, at least I was till you came in and saved me."

"Did I save the day?" Scarlett asked.

"Oh, you did."

"I found you."

"You did."

Scarlett's hand was now in her mammy's, and that was lovely. They didn't move. They stayed in the parlour.

"Are you sad now?"

"No, I'm not," said Scarlett's mammy. "Sure, I'm never sad with you around."

"Why were you sad?"

"I was thinking of my own mammy."

"The one that died long ago."

"That's right," she said. "'Twas long ago. But when I come here— Well, this used to be home, didn't it? Before I wandered up to Dublin. So…"

"Were you sad about the lost baby as well?" Scarlett asked her mammy.

Her mammy's smile was still there.

"I was," she said.

Scarlett's mammy had lost a baby. Scarlett had heard people whispering that in the kitchen – the kitchen at home, in Dublin, where they lived when they weren't on their holidays. *She lost the baby. She's after losing the baby*. It had happened long ago, when Scarlett was so small, she was able to stand in the kitchen for ages before anyone noticed her. Her mammy wasn't there but that hadn't worried her because her daddy was. Sometimes that was how it happened – he was there and she wasn't, or she was there when he wasn't. But now, standing against the table, nearly *under* the table, she heard about the lost baby. The lady from next door, a hairy woman called Missis McLoughlin who made lovely cakes and scones – she had just whispered it. *She's after losing the baby, God love her*. And Scarlett noticed something: her daddy wasn't there now. And who, she wanted to know, was the lost baby? And how could her mammy have lost a baby when Scarlett had never even seen the baby, and she was always – nearly always – with her mammy?

But she said nothing.

She stayed there and she listened.

Then the women saw her.

"You're awake."

"Is mammy finding the baby?"

"What?"

"Oh, God love her."

They gave her biscuits and let her watch the telly

for much longer than ever before, and then her daddy came home by himself and he explained all about the lost baby after all the neighbours had gone back to their own houses.

"Your mammy was going to have a baby," he said, when there was just the two of them. "But now she isn't."

"Why not?"

"She had a thing called a miscarriage."

"What's that?"

"It's when the baby stops growing in her tummy."

"Why?"

"I don't know," he said. "It just happens. Sometimes."

"Where is it lost?"

"What?"

"Missis McLoughlin said the baby was lost," said Scarlett. "I heard her."

"Oh," said Scarlett's dad. "That's a phrase. A way of saying it. It doesn't mean the baby's actually lost. It just won't be born. It won't become a baby."

"I want a baby."

"Yes."

"A sister or a brother."

"Grand."

"Especially a brother."

"Okay."

"When's Mammy coming home?"

"Tomorrow."

"Is she in the hospital?"

"Yes."

"Is she lost?"

"No. She's grand. She's tired. And sad."

Now, Scarlett was bigger and she'd be starting real school when the summer was over. The milking parlour began to feel a bit cold, like it always did after a while. Scarlett and her mammy both shivered, together, while they were still holding hands. It made them laugh.

Scarlett saw her mammy looking around.

"What are you looking for?"

"I thought I felt something," said her mammy.

"There's nothing in here," said Scarlett. "What?"

"Nothing."

"What did you feel?"

"Nothing," said her mammy. "I just – no."

"What?"

"No, it's just—"

"Tell me. Mammy, you have to."

"I thought I heard someone else laughing when we were laughing."

"There's no one here."

"I know that."

"I want to go now. Come on."

"Good idea."

They walked outside, into the sun, and the little bumps on Scarlett's arm, the bumps that were made by the cold, disappeared. They went back inside her skin.

"Did you really hear someone laughing?"

"No," said her mammy. "I couldn't have. It was the echo of us laughing, that's all. Do you agree?"

"Yes," said Scarlett. "That's all it was."

"That's that explained, so. You must be hungry."

"Yes, I am."

"You had a great ol' sleep."

"Yes, I did."

They were walking back across the yard, to the house. Scarlett could feel the sun, like it was patting her head. She liked it. Her mammy called it "the Wexford touch".

Her mammy always walked quite fast across the yard.

"Why don't you like the greyhounds?" Scarlett asked.

"Oh, God," said her mammy. "Sure, I never did like them. I never did. They were too big."

"But so are you," said Scarlett.

Her mammy stopped, and laughed.

"True for you, girl," she said.

Scarlett watched her mammy put her hand over her eyes, like the peak of a cap, so she didn't have to squint. She was looking at the greyhounds behind the fence.

"So," she said. "You want to know why I don't like the greyhounds, even though I'm a bit of a greyhound myself. Is that it?"

She barked, and Scarlett laughed.

"Yes," said Scarlett. "Why? You're bigger than them."

"Well," said her mammy. "This might sound mad. And a little bit sad."

She bent down, so her face was right in front of Scarlett's.

"I blamed the greyhounds for killing my mother."

Scarlett wanted to run.

"Did they—?"

"No, no, they didn't," said her mammy. "It was the flu. It's grand. I know that. But, you see, I always thought if my mother had come into the house with me she'd have been fine. But she didn't. She went and fed the hounds. And I always thought the hounds gave her the flu."

She smiled.

"Mad," she said. "But I couldn't help it. I had to blame something and I'd never liked them anyway. Let's get you fed and washed."

"Just fed."

"Alright," said her mammy. "You've caught me at a soft moment."

She bent down again to Scarlett. "I love being with you," she said.

"I know," said Scarlett.

"I was younger than you when my mother died."

"I know."

"It's always sad."

"I know."

"I decided to blame the hounds," said her mammy. "Because everyone kept telling me not to blame myself. You see, I'd had the flu as well."

"Everybody gets the flu," said Scarlett.

"That's very true," said her mammy. "You're a wise one. But back then it was more serious. People died. My mother died."

"She didn't die," said Scarlett. "She just went away."

"God," said her mammy. "Where did you hear that?"

"Nowhere," said Scarlett. "It was just in my head."

Her mammy bent down and kissed the top of Scarlett's head.

"There."

They went into the kitchen.

"Did you live in the pig shed after you died?" Scarlett asked Tansey.

"I did not, faith," said Tansey. "Sure, why would I want to live in the pig shed? Even if I am dead and I can't smell anything."

They were still in the kitchen.

"I just always thought it was spooky," said Scarlett.

"That's not a very nice thing to say, Mammy," said Mary.

"What?!"

"You said Tansey was spooky," said Mary. "She's, like, your granny, after all."

"I said the pig shed was spooky!"

"Because Tansey was in it."

"But she wasn't!" said Scarlett. "She just said so!"

"But you thought—"

"Ah now stop that, girls," said Tansey. "You'd wake the dead. And I'm the proof of that."

"Sorry."

"So, look," said Tansey. "It was bad enough dying – it wasn't nice at all, I'll tell you that for nothing. But leaving Emer alone like that – well, I couldn't do it. My husband—"

She looked at Scarlett.

"Your granddad," she said, "was a lovely man and he did his best. And he did it very well. As reliable as the rain. He was a daddy *and* a mammy to Emer. And there was his mother as well and she was grand. But, still, I couldn't go. I had to stay. Until she became a mammy, herself. And even then I couldn't let go. I was always worried she'd—"

"Tansey?" said Mary.

"Yes, dear?" said Tansey.

"Granny's in hospital."

"I know she is," said Tansey. "And that's why I'm here."

She sighed. "I've been lingering," she said. "That word again. She was so little, you see – I couldn't leave her. I was just so anxious. I still am."

Then Scarlett spoke.

"We're going to see my mother – Emer – now," she said. "Do you want to come?"

"Yes," said Tansey. "I'd like that."

She sat up.

"But I can't."

"Why can't you?" Mary asked.

"Well," said Tansey. "Look at me. I'm a ghost."

"So?"

"The last thing a hospital needs is a ghost wandering around," said Tansey. "All the heart attacks – can you imagine? Believe me, dear. Sick people don't want to see ghosts."

"But the hospital's, like, horrible already," said Mary. "No one would notice you. I mean, like – I don't mean you're horrible. You're not. But most of the people in there look like they've been seeing ghosts all their lives. Some of them *are* ghosts. Do ghosts smoke?"

"No," said Tansey. "Unfortunately."

"Why would you want to smoke?" Mary asked.

"I wouldn't," said Tansey. "But I'd love to be able to cough. A good ol' cough now. That'd be grand. I'd love my lungs back."

She smiled.

"Don't mind me," she said. "Smoking's a filthy habit. It's not good for a dead person to be around with the living too much. You're making me jealous. With your *lungs*."

She said it in a way that made Mary and Scarlett laugh.

"I'd love to see Emer," said Tansey. "She's frightened, isn't she?"

"Yes," said Scarlett.

"I can help, you see," said Tansey. "I can – well – I can be her mother."

She smiled. "Then I can go."

"Go where?" Mary asked.

"Well," said Tansey. "Where I should have been these years."

"Oh. Yeah," said Mary.

"'Oh yeah' is right, girl," said Tansey.

She smiled again.

"You can't cry," said Mary.

"No."

"But you can smile. How come?"

Tansey laughed.

"I'm not being cheeky," Mary told her mother. "Just in case you think I am."

"I don't!"

"I don't know the answer to that one," said Tansey. "I never thought of it till now. I can laugh as well. Although it's years since I did."

"Did you laugh in the milking parlour once?" asked Scarlett.

"Oh, I laughed in that parlour a lot more than once," said Tansey. "Many's the time I laughed in the milking parlour."

"After you died," said Scarlett. "Long after. When I was a little girl."

"No."

"My mother thought she heard someone else laughing one day, besides us."

"It wasn't me."

"Are you sure?"

"No."

"It might have been you."

"It might."

She sighed. "I died young but I've an old one's memory. I recall some things precisely and other important things are gone. I might have played hurling for Wexford, for all I know."

"You didn't."

"I'm not surprised. Your granddad did."

"I know."

Tansey looked at Mary.

"I'd love to talk to Emer," she said. "I want to tell her there's nothing to worry about. Dying's not so bad. Especially when you're old. And she's had a great life, after all. Lovely daughter, and grandchildren."

Scarlett was crying now.

"I'm sorry, dear," said Tansey.

"No," said Scarlett. "It's fine. She always spoke about you when I was growing up. Even though she couldn't remember much. I think it would be great if you met her. Although, it's all a bit strange."

"Yep," said Mary. "It's definitely weird. I'm not being cheeky."

"Just because you say you're not being cheeky doesn't mean you aren't," said Scarlett.

"But I'm not," said Mary. "It *is* weird. It's *so* weird. How many other ghosts do you, like, know?"

Scarlett shrugged. "I don't know," she said.

"Now I'm scared," said Mary.

"Only one," said Tansey. "You know only the one, and that's me."

"Why can't you not come into the hospital?"

"I'm not good under the light bulbs, you see," said Tansey. "You saw that yourself. I *fade*. It wouldn't be fair. Sure, people in hospitals are frightened enough already without ghosts marching up the corridors. But there's one thing—"

"What?"

"If the ghost holds a child's hand—"

She looked at Mary.

"I'm not a child," said Mary.

"Yes, you are!" said her mother.

"I'm not," said Mary. "You said so."

"When?!"

"Yesterday," said Mary. "When I said I didn't want to clean my room. You said I had to because, and I quote, *You're not a little girl any more*."

"That's right!" said Scarlett. "You're not a little girl! But you *are* a child!"

"Why am I?" said Mary. "Because you say so?"

"Yes!"

"A-hem."

It was Tansey. "Now, ladies," she said. "Ghosts don't usually have to imitate a cough, to get attention."

"I'm not a child," Mary whispered.

"Yes, you are!" her mother whispered back.

"Not!"

"Ah, stop that, the pair of you," said Tansey. "And listen to me now."

"Sorry."

"If the ghost holds the hand of a child," said Tansey, "as they walk into a building—"

"Like a hospital."

"Exactly," said Tansey. "The ghost becomes more solid. But only if she's holding the hand of a child."

"How does it work?" asked Mary.

"I don't know," said Tansey.

"Did you ever try it?"

"No."

"How did you find out about it then?"

"I just seem to know," said Tansey.

"And you're sure it'll work?"

"I'm not, no."

"I'm not convinced," said Mary. "It sounds a bit, like, superstitious."

"I'm a ghost," said Tansey. "And I'm probably, *like*, a bit of a superstition. But I'm here, all the same."

"Okay."

"Will we try it, so?"

"Okay."

Scarlett shouted at the kitchen ceiling.

"Boys?!"

They heard a noise from upstairs.

"I think one of them said 'What?'," said Mary.

"We're going back to the hospital!" shouted Scarlett. "Your dad will be home soon!"

They heard another noise.

"I think one of them said 'Okay'," said Mary.

She didn't want to sleep.

"I'm alive."

Her eyes would close. She couldn't help it. She just couldn't keep her eyes open.

I'm alive.

It was after eight o'clock, and dark. Mary and Tansey sat in the back of the car, outside the house and under one of the trees.

"Don't forget your safety belt," said Mary.

"What's a safety belt?" Tansey asked.

Mary showed her the belt, and how to put it on.

"Now," Tansey asked, "does a ghost really need a safety belt?"

But she clicked the belt buckle into place. Mary watched, half-expecting the belt to go right through Tansey's body. But it didn't. It went across her chest and lap.

"You're kind of solid already," she said.

"I am," said Tansey. "That'll be all the spuds I ate when I was a young one. But, d'you know what?" she said, as Scarlett started the car – and the light inside the car went off. "I've never been in a car before."

"No way," said Mary.

Tansey was even clearer in the dark. Everything about her looked real and alive.

"It's true," she said. "There were very few cars back in my day. And they were all black."

Scarlett turned on to the main road to the hospital. The rush hour was over and there was hardly any traffic.

"We'll be there in no time!" said Scarlett.

"Whatever that means," said Mary, quietly.

She watched Tansey looking out the car window, at the houses and rows of shops, at the other cars and street lights.

"It's better than walking," said Tansey.

"That's what I keep telling Mammy," said Mary. "But she won't listen to me."

"Walking is great!" said Scarlett.

"It did me no good," said Tansey, quietly to Mary.

She sat up straight. "I like this car business," she said. "It's like being at the films."

They drove into the hospital car park. Scarlett found an empty space, and parked. She looked back over the car seat at Mary and Tansey.

"So!"

"We're there, are we?" said Tansey.

"We are!"

"Grand."

They got out of the car.

"So!" said Scarlett, again. She looked nervous.

Mary walked around to the other side of the car and took Tansey's hand in hers.

"It's cold," she said. "I'm not being cheeky."

"I know you're not," said Tansey.

Mary squeezed Tansey's hand, a little bit. "But it's nice," she said.

"Oh good."

"And a bit weird."

"You're being cheeky now, are you?"

"Yes."

"We'd better get a move on!" said Scarlett.

Visiting time was nearly over.

"Wait now," said Tansey.

She let go of Mary's hand and stood under one of the strip lights that lit the car park.

"Can you see me?"

"Hardly," said Mary.

It was a bit horrible, because Tansey seemed to be disappearing, even breaking up. Mary ran to her and held her hand.

"Good girl yourself," said Tansey. "Am I any clearer now?" she asked Scarlett.

"I think so!" said Scarlett. "But – I don't know! Maybe I'm just being biased."

"But can you see me?"

"Well, yes."

"Will we chance it, so?" Tansey asked Mary.

"Cool," said Mary. "But what'll happen if it doesn't work?"

"Oh, dozens of people will have heart attacks," said Tansey. "But, sure, it's a hospital, so they'll be grand. I don't like this car park place at all."

The car park was an ugly, bare building, with no windows or colour.

"How do we get out?" said Tansey.

"There's a lift."

"A what?"

The lift was broken, so they went down the stairs. Tansey stayed close to the wall, away from the lights. They met no one coming up as they went down, to the exit, or on the footpath that led to the front of the hospital.

They stayed on the grass, away from the lamps that dropped big circles of light on to the path. It was busier here. A lot of people were leaving the hospital and coming towards them. There were groups of sad looking people, different ages, families, after visiting people they loved and had had to leave inside. There were other people walking alone, their heads down, tired. No one paid much attention to this different family group, daughter, mother and dead great-granny, as they went what seemed the wrong way at this time of night.

"So far, so good!"

But they were coming up to the main entrance. They'd have to step off the grass and walk under the fluorescent light, into the hospital foyer. It was so bright in there, it looked as if the windows had been painted in white gloss paint.

Tansey stopped.

"It'll take more than a child's hand to get me through all this brightness," she said.

"I'm not a child," said Mary.

"Right, so," said Tansey. "Here goes."

They held hands tight and walked off the grass, towards the people in dressing gowns and slippers who stood, or sat in wheelchairs, around the entrance, chatting and coughing, sighing and laughing. Tansey's fingers got no warmer in Mary's grip. But Mary stopped noticing because all she could think of was the people at the entrance, and their faces. She didn't look at Tansey – she was afraid to. It was really bright here, brighter than a normal day. It was a horrible, headachy light that seemed to burn the colours out of clothes and hair. Everything was grey. Mary began to think that Tansey would get past these people, because everyone looked so grey and ghostlike – when she heard the gasp.

There was a man with no legs, in a wheelchair, sitting away from the light. He was staring at something right beside Mary. His mouth was wide open. His cigarette was clinging to his lip. He hadn't lit it yet and the flame from his lighter had started to singe his beard.

"A ghost."

Mary didn't hear him, but she knew that they were the words he'd just whispered.

This time she looked.

Tansey was shimmering. Mary could see right through her, even though she was holding Tansey's hand and it still felt cold and solid. It might have *felt* cold and solid but it almost wasn't there. Tansey was disappearing. The man in the wheelchair hadn't said anything else. But Mary felt Tansey's fingers slip from hers.

Other men and women were looking now, staring at where Tansey had been standing. Their expressions were much more puzzled than frightened.

"Keep going!" said Scarlett.

"But—"

"Act normal, Mary!"

Act normal? Mary didn't know what "normal" meant. She'd just been holding the hand of the ghost of a woman who'd died in 1928, who seemed to have evaporated just as Mary was getting to know her. She was being stared at by a man with no legs and a burning beard – and other people were staring at her too.

She wanted to cry.

But she kept walking. Her mother grabbed the hand that Tansey had been holding. Usually, Mary wouldn't have let her mother do that. She was too old for it. But her mother's hand was warm, and the hand, the fingers, told her: her mother needed Mary now – and Mary needed her mother.

They walked through the smoke and stares. Mary wanted to look back, to see if she could see Tansey, or a hint of Tansey. But she didn't look. The entrance doors slid open and they went straight in, still holding hands.

She looked at the little girl playing at the well. The little girl, her daughter. The little girl was dropping pebbles, leaning over to hear how long it took before she heard the pebble smack the black water down below.

A little girl, but she was getting bigger by the day. She'd grown out of the green coat. Tansey saw her wearing a new coat one day, the start of the winter days. Tansey knew it was winter by the slant of the sun – because she didn't feel the cold. She wished she could, but she couldn't. She saw Emer in the new coat and two feelings ripped through her at once, pride and a dead woman's heartache. Emer was growing up – she was already tall and she'd the long legs of a foal – and Tansey could only watch. The new coat was somebody else's choice. The day out to buy it, the trip to Enniscorthy or even Wexford, the adventure of the day, all the things Tansey had been looking forward to – gone, stopped, never there.

She couldn't go near her. She wouldn't – she'd never frighten Emer. Tansey was dead. She was dead three winters. But she couldn't go.

It was a sad little face, searching for good pebbles. Four of the greyhounds were staring at her, through the fence. But Emer never looked their way. She had a way of avoiding them – she didn't even have to think about it. She could move around and look everywhere, except at the dogs.

She'd found the stone she wanted. Tansey could see, it was bigger than the others. Emer wiped her nose on her sleeve. A mother's job, to make sure she had a hankie. She watched Emer go back over to the well. She watched her lean over. She watched one leg rise off the ground. She waited for Emer to drop the stone into the well. But she didn't. The one foot came down, then both feet were off the ground and Tansey knew this was different, this was bad.

She went over the yard, fast, and through the fence, straight in among the greyhounds. They saw nothing but they knew she was there – and they went wild. They bit at the air and tumbled over themselves and created a riot that had Jim's mother charging out the back door in a second. She grabbed Emer up off the well and carried her away from it.

Emer was protesting.

"I wasn't falling in! I was not!"

"My heart!" said Jim's mother.

"I was only dropping the stones."

"You scamp, I told you."

"I wasn't falling in!"

"But for the hounds you'd be drowned."

"I hate them."

"They saved you."

"They didn't! I saved myself!"

Tansey was back across the yard, in the shade of the milking parlour. She could only watch, and she could only wish that the angry words were being shouted at her. She watched Emer follow her grandmother, in the back door. She watched the door being closed.

"Granny?"

Mary watched her granny's eyes.

"Granny?"

The eyes opened.

"You're back, are you?"

"I am," said Mary, and she thought she sounded like Tansey.

"Did you come on your own, did you?"

"No," said Mary.

"Where's your mammy then?"

"She's talking to a doctor."

"Oh, she shouldn't be talking to those fellas. They don't know the half of what they think they know."

"She's asking if we can, like, take you out," said Mary.

"Ah now," said her granny. "I don't know if I'd be up to a trip to the zoo or the seaside. If that's the kind of 'out' you mean."

Her head moved on the pillow, and her shoulders. She tried to sit up. "But d'you know what?" she said. "It's lovely to see you, anyway. You're a bit of a tonic."

"I'm a gin and a tonic?"

"You are indeed," said Emer.

Mary helped her with one of the pillows. She put it behind her granny's back.

"Now," said her granny. "So she's talking to one of the doctors, is she?"

"Yes."

"The big fella?"

"No," said Mary. "A woman."

"Oh," said her granny. "Grand."

She looked carefully at Mary. "But I'm really not well, you know," she said, quietly, seriously.

"I know," said Mary. "We know."

"We know," her granny repeated. "So, why do *we* want to get me out of this bed?"

Mary thought about this.

"To meet someone," she said.

"Oh."

"Someone special."

"Oh," said her granny. "Someone special. That'll be Elvis, will it?"

She smiled.

"Better," said Mary.

"Better than Elvis?"

They were joking, but it was a serious conversation. They were often like that, Mary and her granny, when they were alone together.

"Yes," said Mary. "Like, way better."

Scarlett came into the room. She sat on the bed.

"The doctor says fine," she told Mary – and Emer.

"Fine what?" said Emer.

"It's fine for us to take you out for a little while," said Scarlett. "So. Well, Mammy. Is there one more adventure in you?"

"Adventure?"

"Yes."

"Are you serious?"

"Yes."

Emer closed her eyes and opened them again, as if to make sure that Mary and Scarlett were still real and there.

"Well now," she said. "I think there just might be one more small adventure left in me. And it'll be nice to get away from all the coughs and splutters."

She sat up properly, for the first time in more than a week.

"God, now," she said. "I felt that."

She pulled back the sheet.

"Look at the skinny legs on me," she said. "I'm like a chicken on a supermarket shelf."

"No, you're not!"

"Cluck cluck."

Emer brought her legs to the side of the bed, and let them drop. Her toes nearly touched the floor.

"I'm still lanky Emer," she said. "Bring your shoulder over here now," she said to Mary.

Mary stood right beside her granny. Emer put her hand on Mary's shoulder.

"You've grown again," she said.

"Have I?" said Mary.

"You have."

"Cool."

Emer held on to Mary's shoulder, and stood.

"God now," she said. "I haven't been this high in months."

She took a step. Mary went with her.

"Good girl."

She took another step.

"Nothing to it."

And another.

"Oh boy."

And another.

"Are you alright?" Scarlett asked.

"I'm grand," said Emer.

She leaned on Mary.

"I'm grand. But I'll be needing one of those chairs with the wheels for the rest of the journey, wherever it is we're headed. The ol' legs are rattling here."

"There's a wheelchair right behind you!"

"Lovely," said Emer. "A Rolls-Royce, I hope."

She held on to Mary's shoulder – Mary could feel her granny's fingers through her hoodie, and she thought her granny felt nervous – as she lowered herself into the wheelchair.

"There now," said Emer. "I landed safely."

The nice nurse was walking past the door.

"You're off out," she said.

"I am," said Emer.

"Somewhere nice?"

"Ah now," said Emer. "Anywhere's nice with this gang."

"Be sure to wrap up," said the nurse. "It's a cranky enough night out there."

Scarlett put a blanket over Emer's legs.

"That's nice," said Emer.

Mary and Scarlett collected what they thought Emer might need to bring, her dressing gown, her purse, her handbag, her slippers, her coat and a cardigan.

Mary got down on her knees in front of the wheelchair.

"Don't run over me, Granny."

She put the slippers on Emer's feet while Scarlett wrapped the dressing gown around Emer's shoulders.

"Lovely," said Emer. "Why are we doing this again?"

"You're meeting someone," said Mary.

"Oh, that's right," said Emer. "I remember. Who?"

"Someone special."

"That's right."

"Someone who really wants to meet you."

"Grand," said Emer. "But I'm too old to be getting married again, you know."

Scarlett laughed.

"Ready?!"

"Anchors away," said Emer.

12

Ghosts don't sleep.

But sometimes they close their eyes.

Tansey's eyes were closed when she heard the car door being unlocked. She opened them, and saw Mary's face.

"How did you get in without the key?" Mary asked.

"Ah sure," said Tansey. "It's one of the tricks. I thought it best to stay hidden away in here. And I like it."

She could see Scarlett's face now, looking over Mary's shoulder. Then Mary and Scarlett stepped out of the way. And Tansey saw a new face.

The new face stared back at Tansey.

"Emer?" said Tansey.

"What?"

"You're Emer," said Tansey.

"I know I am," said Emer.

Scarlett and Mary were there again, at the open back door of the car, on either side of Emer in the wheelchair. Tansey watched as her daughter, her ancient daughter, put one hand on the arm of the wheelchair and the other on Mary's shoulder. Then she watched her stand up. Her face, her head, disappeared for a while. Then it was back, big and getting bigger, as Emer, helped by Mary, slid into the back seat, beside Tansey. They could hear Scarlett at the back of the car as she tried to fold the wheelchair and put it into the boot.

"I can't do it!" they heard her.

"Let me try," they heard Mary.

"I think you press this thing here!"

"Mind your fingers."

"I am – ouch!"

Tansey and Emer looked at each other.

"Do you recognize me, Emer?" Tansey asked.

Emer looked. She looked, and saw – it happened slowly. The face was hazy, as if it was hidden behind a mask made of very thin material. The material got thinner and thinner. And Emer knew who she was looking at.

She spoke very quietly.

"I think I know you," she said.

"Good girl."

"You're my mother."

"Yes," said Tansey.

"Have you come to collect me?"

"Not yet," said Tansey. "There's no hurry."

"But you're dead."

"I am."

They heard the boot being slammed. Then Scarlett and Mary walked past them and, at exactly the same time, opened the front doors of the car and climbed in. Then they sat there quietly, almost afraid to turn around and look at the women behind them. Nothing was said, and they couldn't hear breathing.

Then Emer spoke.

"You're a ghost, so."

"I am."

"In the back of a car."

"Yes."

"That's a new one," said Emer. "I never saw that in any of the films. A ghost in a car."

They were quiet again, for a while – for too long.

"Will we go for a drive?!" said Scarlett.

She looked into the rear-view mirror and saw her mother, but not Tansey.

"Is she gone?!"

She turned quickly, and saw Tansey looking straight at her. Scarlett screamed – and everyone else in the car seemed to scream. They all screamed once but the screams were trapped inside the car, so they bounced and ricocheted and were still there when the laughing started.

"I got such a shock!" said Scarlett. "Sorry!"

"Was it the mirror business?" Tansey asked her.

"Yes!" said Scarlett. "I couldn't see you!"

"Ghosts can't be seen in mirrors, Mammy," Mary told her. "They have no reflections. Or shadows."

"Oh," said Scarlett. "I didn't know."

"Sure, everyone knows that," said Emer.

"Well, I didn't!"

"Well, then you should," said Emer. "And not be screaming like that and scaring the wits out of us all."

"Emer," said Tansey.

"What?"

"Stop being so rude," said Tansey. "Say you're sorry."

"I will not, faith," said Emer. "Why should I?"

"I'm your mother," said Tansey. "So go on now, do what you're told. Say sorry."

"I'm sorry, Scarlett," said Emer.

"This is weird," said Mary. "And I am *so* not being cheeky."

"What's weird about it?" Emer asked.

She tried to lean forward, so she could see Mary's face properly. But she couldn't.

"Well, for a start," said Mary. "Your mother's younger than mine."

"You're only jealous," said Emer. "But I can see your point, all the same."

She looked at Tansey.

"Are you really a ghost?"

"Oh, I am."

"And you're really my mother?"

"Yes," said Tansey. "I am."

"I'll tell you what's really weird then," said Emer. "I'm not all that surprised."

"And that makes it even weirder," said Mary.

"That's true, I suppose," said Emer.

The car park had emptied while they'd been sitting there. The last of the hospital visitors had driven away and there were only a few empty cars left, in a space designed for hundreds.

"We'll go somewhere!" said Scarlett. "Will we?"

She turned the key in the ignition, then stopped.

"I don't want to be pushy," she said.

"I don't want to stay here," said Mary. "It's spooky. I'm not being cheeky."

"Where will we go?" Scarlett asked.

"I'm hungry," said Mary.

"Are you hungry, Mammy?" said Scarlett.

"No," said Emer.

"I wish I was," said Tansey.

"So, where will we go?"

Emer tried to lean forward again, and this time she managed it. Her face was at Mary's shoulder.

"I want to go to Wexford," she said.

"Wexford!"

"Wexford," said Emer. "The farm. That's what I want to see and that's where I want to go."

She fell back into her seat.

"But it's such a long drive!" said Scarlett. "And it's dark and quite late already and—"

"I want to go there as well," said Tansey.

"But I told Doctor Patel that we'd bring Mammy – Emer – back in an hour!"

"I want to go to Wexford too," said Mary.

"But the farm doesn't belong to the family any more!"

"I only want to see it," said Emer. "Sure, I don't want to rob their cattle."

"You're being cheeky again, Emer," said Tansey.

"Sorry, Scarlett, love."

"Oh-kay!" said Scarlett. "Let's go to Wexford!"

"Cool," said Mary.

Scarlett started the car. Before she took her foot off the brake, she and Mary heard a voice behind them.

"I have to go pee."

"Who said that?!"

"Ghosts don't pee, dear," said Tansey.

Mary sat up a bit, so she could see in the rear-view mirror. She could only see her granny. There was no hint of Tansey back there. She didn't turn around. She kept looking in the mirror.

"Do you have to go pee, Granny?" she asked, as she watched her granny's eyes closing. The car was dark but there was a fluorescent light on the low ceiling of the car park, just behind the car's rear window, so Mary could see her granny perfectly. She'd fallen asleep.

"Put your belt on, Mary!" said Scarlett.

"In a sec."

Mary's granny was asleep and she was leaning against something that Mary couldn't see – as if an invisible hand was stopping her from falling sideways. And there was something else. Mary looked at one of her granny's hands. It looked like it was in mid-air, and holding something that Mary couldn't see.

She turned now, and saw it. Her granny's hand was on Tansey's lap and holding Tansey's hand.

"That is so cool," said Mary.

Tansey smiled at her.

Mary put on her safety belt.

It was quiet. Scarlett just drove. Mary looked out the window. She didn't ask for music or food. Her granny was asleep and she knew it was special, this trip. It was something that hadn't been planned. It was actually impossible. Four generations of women – "I'm a *woman*," Mary said to herself – heading off on a journey in a car. One of them dead, one of them dying, one of them driving, one of them just beginning. *I'm a woman*. She looked out the window and knew where she was, for a while. They were driving beside the sea, still in Dublin. The lights lit places and buildings she'd seen before. The big chimneys of the power station were behind them, and they'd just passed one of those things, a Martello tower, that had been built when Napoleon Bonaparte or someone like that had been thinking of invading

Ireland – or something. The name of this place came into her head. Sandymount.

Then the sea was gone and they were on a motorway – Mary could tell by the way her mother put her foot on the pedal and made the car go much faster. She didn't know where they were any more. The road was everything for a while. There was nothing else to look at in the dark.

"No corners."

"Who spoke?!"

"I did," said Emer.

"You're awake!"

"That's good to know."

Mary was suddenly aware: she'd been asleep. She was awake now, though – definitely. Her granny's voice had woken her – she thought.

She turned, so she could see her granny.

"What did you say, Granny?" she asked.

"No corners," said Emer.

"What d'you mean, like?"

"I mean, there aren't any corners on the road," said Emer. "And there should be. Are we going the right way at all?"

"Yes!"

"Where's Ashford, so?" said Emer.

"It's bypassed!" said Scarlett.

"It's what?"

"Bypassed!"

"My God."

They were quiet for a while.

"Are there no corners at all any more, Scarlett?"

"No!" said Scarlett. "At least, I don't think so. It's straight all the way. Sorry."

Tansey spoke now, for the first time in ages.

"I always liked a good corner," she said.

"Ah sure, stop," said Emer. "There's nothing like a good corner."

"You never know what you're going to get."

"Now you're talking … Mammy."

Mary heard the two women behind her giggling.

"What's so funny?"

"Me," said Emer. "Calling this one here 'Mammy'. It's gas."

"She *is* your mammy."

"I know," said Emer. "But it's still gas. Sure, I'm eighty-something, I forget how much. And this one here's well over a hundred."

"I am."

Mary smiled, but she began to worry as she watched her granny's eyes start to close again. There was something about it – even in the dark, or maybe because of the dark. Her granny's face seemed to close too, as her eyes closed. As if she'd stopped being her granny, or anyone. But she kept looking, even though it was awkward, trying to look behind her while the car was moving fast and she was strapped in. She wanted to see something first, something to reassure her, a yawn or a little twitch, something to tell her that her granny was just asleep.

"We should maybe have waited till daylight," said Tansey. "There's nothing to look at."

"Only the dark," said Emer, her eyes still shut.

Mary laughed and turned around, to face forward again.

"Where would we be now, if there was anything to look at?" Tansey asked.

"We're going past Arklow!" said Scarlett.

"Thank God for that," said Emer. "That's one town I'll happily bypass."

"We're not too far, so," said Tansey.

"No!"

No one spoke after that.

For a good while.

There were farmhouses, away off the road. It was nearly midnight and most of the windows were dark but there were some lights on, over the front doors. Mary started to count them until she got to seven, and there was a gap and she forgot that she'd been doing it.

"Gorey!"

"Where?"

"We're going past it."

"Which side?"

"I don't know!" said Scarlett.

"That's just daft," said Tansey. "Can you not go into Gorey any more, only past it?"

"You *can* go in!" said Scarlett. "You just go off this road."

"I used to work in Gorey," said Tansey. "'Twas in Gorey I met Jim. Emer's father."

"Do you want to go through Gorey?!"

"No," said Tansey. "It wouldn't be the same. I'm better off not looking."

"Ah now, Gorey isn't too bad," said Emer.

The women in the back were giggling again. This time Mary didn't look. The giggling stopped and it was quiet again, just the wheels on the road – there was no other sound that Mary could hear, till her mother sighed. Mary looked, and watched her mother yawning.

"Tired?"

"No!"

"Liar."

"Oh," said Scarlett. "Look!"

They were coming to the end of the long straight road. There was a roundabout ahead. It felt like years since the car had slowed. Mary could feel it in her chest as she was pressed, very slightly, against her safety belt.

"Are we there?"

"Not yet!"

They could see the shape of Enniscorthy ahead of them, the cathedral and, over the river, the blunt top of Vinegar Hill.

"Oh, look," said Tansey. "The castle's still there."

"Course it is," said Emer.

They drove slowly through the town.

"There's more of it than in my day," said Tansey. "More buildings and corners."

"No harm."

"But it's still the town."

"It is."

"A good ol' town."

"Not the worst."

They crossed the river.

"What's the river called?" Mary asked.

"The Slaney!"

"It's the exact same, the river."

"I'd say the water's new."

"True."

"Nearly there!"

"Oh, we know," said Tansey. "We know. We're on the home stretch, alright."

"I'd know it off by heart," said Emer. "Every little swerve."

"Me too!" said Scarlett.

"Why don't I know it?" Mary asked.

"What do you mean?!'

"Like, you all know the way," said Mary. "But I don't. I've heard about it, the farm like, but I've never been there. Have I?"

"No, you haven't!"

"Why not?"

"It was sold."

"Why?"

"No one left to farm it," said her granny, behind her. "James the Baby never married. I think he was afraid to. The granny was a great woman but she could be a bit fierce."

"But Tansey lived there with her!" said Scarlett. "Didn't you, Tansey?"

"I did," said Tansey. "But, then, I was a bit fierce myself."

"The fierceness came as the granny got older," said Emer.

"That's often the way," said Tansey.

"Anyway," said Emer. "I don't think James the Baby thought he could bring another woman into the house. And by the time she died, sure, poor James the Baby was getting old himself."

She coughed, once.

"God now, I'm exhausted after all that talk," she said.

"Who called him James the Baby?" Mary asked.

"What?"

"All of us did," said Emer. "That was his name."

"James the *Baby*, like?"

"He was always James the Baby."

"And you expected someone to, like, marry him? A man called James the Baby?"

There was silence in the car.

"I can see your point, alright," said Emer. "Now. Poor James."

Scarlett spoke, after they'd all stopped laughing.

"Who bought the farm?!"

"What?"

"Who bought the farm?!"

"I can't remember."

"I used to know the name!" said Scarlett. "I think it was—"

"I remember now," said Emer. "It was the Furlongs."

"They had the farm up the lane!"

"They did," said Tansey. "Coolnamana."

"That's the one," said Emer.

"And they bought our farm, did they?"

"They did," said Emer. "There was Ollie Furlong had four sons. And poor James the Baby – sorry, James the Man – who used to play the hurling with Ollie, was all by himself and no one to work for him. And he broke his arm, you see. He was always breaking some bone or other, was James the Man. So—"

"He sold it to Ollie Furlong."

"No," said Emer. "Not for a long while. He kept it up, he loved the farm. But then, only when it was too much for him. He gave it up. It was sad."

"Where did he live?" Mary asked.

"He stayed on in the house," said Emer. "But then, sure, he died."

"Nearly there!"

"It's a grand wide road."

"Who lives there now?"

"I don't know," said Emer. "A Furlong, I suppose. Or someone belonging to a Furlong."

"Or no one at all."

"Empty?" said Tansey. "No, it couldn't be. It was a grand house. There'd have to be someone in it."

"And," said Mary, "we're, like, dropping in for a chat after midnight, are we?"

"It *is* a bit odd!"

"They'll set the dogs on us," said Tansey.

Mary heard a little yelp. She turned and saw her granny – or, her granny's face – and the terror that had taken over her.

"There there," said Tansey, and Mary watched her as she patted Emer's arm. "We won't do it. What sort of eejits are we at all? Thinking we can go knocking on a stranger's door in the middle of the night."

"We could wait till it's bright."

"Where?"

"In the car!"

"It'll be hours, sure," said Emer. "And another thing."

"What's that, dear?"

"I don't want to be marching through a yard full of greyhounds, in the dark or in the daylight. I won't do it – even if I could march."

The car was slowing again. Mary watched her mother turn on the indicator and look in the rear-view mirror as she moved the car off the road, on to the hard shoulder.

"Well!" said her mother. "We'll have to make our minds up! One more minute and we're there!"

She stopped the car. They could see the village right ahead of them.

"So!" said Scarlett. "Are we staying here or going?"

She turned to look back at her mother and dead grandmother at the same time Mary did, and they nearly knocked their heads together. But, actually, their heads hardly touched at all and what Emer and Tansey saw was two faces, squashed in the gap between the front seats, looking at them.

"So," said Mary. "What's it to be?"

They decided to walk.

Scarlett and Tansey did most of the deciding. They'd walk, and that way they'd see the old house and the yard but there'd be no car lights or engines to disturb whoever was sleeping in the house.

"That'll be grand, so," said Tansey.

"Great!"

"There's one problem," said Emer.

"The greyhounds!"

"No. We'll deal with them if they're there."

"Let *me* guess, Granny," said Mary. "You're very sick."

"Oh!" said Scarlett. "I forgot that."

"Actually," said Mary. "You've, like, been in hospital forever. Isn't that right, Granny?"

"Don't rub it in, Mary," said her mother.

"But," said Mary, "how do you propose to get around the granny-can't-walk problem?"

"Simple!" said Scarlett. "I'll just get the wheelchair out of the boot and that should solve the granny-can't-walk problem, I'd say! What do you think, Mary?!"

"Scarlett got you there, lovey," Emer told Mary.

"I forgot about the wheelchair," said Mary. "Sorry for being rude."

"That's fine," said Scarlett.

It was fun for the first couple of minutes, as they walked along the side of the road, into the village. There were street lights, on one side, so they could see everything clearly. The road had been resurfaced a few years before. There were no potholes or cracks. Mary pushed the wheelchair, and it was easy. All they had to do was walk, and push – and talk.

"The church hasn't changed."

"No."

"Look at the shop, though," said Tansey. "Who's this Spar fella? He wasn't around in my day."

"That's the name. They're all over the place. Like Woolworth's, maybe."

"The pub's the same."

"It is."

"I was never in it."

"No more than I was."

"They let the women into the pubs these days, I think."

"I was never in that particular establishment," said Emer. "But I've been into plenty of other pubs."

"Good for you."

Mary listened to her granny and great-granny. She loved the way they spoke, and the way they seemed to bounce off each other. She looked at her mother, and she could tell: she was enjoying it too. They strolled along, the older women at the front and the two younger ones behind them, chatting and listening.

Then they came to the lane.

It wasn't much more than a gap in the hedge, a very narrow road that disappeared quickly into darkness. The smooth surface of the road was gone, and they were on gravel and muck and small holes and the possibility of much bigger ones ahead. The street lights were behind them, and useless once they reached the first of the bends.

"How many bends to the house, Emer?"

"Seven," said Emer. "Unless they're after adding or subtracting a few."

"I'd say it's still the seven," said Tansey.

"I can't see!"

"That's the problem," said Emer.

She tried to turn – so she could look up at Mary.

"And, no offence, Mary. But it's a bumpy ol' ride now that we're off the road. And I'm not liking it a bit."

"Sorry."

"Here goes!" said Scarlett.

"What?"

Scarlett leaned down in front of her mother, and turned. Emer knew immediately what she was expected to do. She put her arms around Scarlett's neck and hung on as Scarlett stood up straight. Scarlett put her hands behind her back, gently grabbed her mother's legs and pulled them to her sides.

"Oh my God," said Emer.

"Alright there, Mammy?!" said Scarlett.

Mary laughed at the sight of her mother giving her granny a piggyback. But, even while she laughed, she felt sad. Her granny had lost so much weight. That was the only reason her mother – her daughter – could carry her.

"Put the wheelchair up on the ditch and we can collect it on our way back."

Her granny shouldn't have been that easy to carry. It was weird and terrible. But it was funny too.

"Gee up there, horsey!" said Emer to Scarlett.

Emer's legs stuck out in front, like the handles of a wheelbarrow. Mary felt a hand touch hers. It was Tansey's. It was very dark, but Mary could see her clearly.

They were all moving again. Mary and Tansey moved to the front and Scarlett and Emer came along behind them.

"This'll be the second bend."

"You're right there," said Tansey. "And if we ignored the bend and kept going straight we'd come up to the Furlongs'."

"That's right. It's coming back to me."

"It never left you."

The ground was very uneven and Mary's feet slapped it because she couldn't judge exactly where her feet were going to land. But she held on to Tansey's hand and that made her feel more surefooted. While she walked beside Tansey she knew she was going the right way.

There were tall hedges on both sides of the lane.

Emer coughed.

"Are you alright there, Emer?" Tansey asked.

"I think I'm after swallowing a leaf," she said.

"Would you like a little rest?"

"Not at all," said Emer. "This is great."

As she spoke, one of the hedges seemed to fall away and they could see much more clearly.

"The low field."

"That's right."

"Exactly where we left it."

Mary could make out the fence, and the field behind it, and the hill that went down to—

"What's that down there?"

"That's a bit of the Slaney."

"The river?"

"The river."

"Cool."

The Slaney was in her geography book. It was one of the major rivers of Ireland and it was flowing near Mary. It flowed past the farm where her granny and her great-granny came from – and, in a way, where Mary came from.

"That's amazing."

"Sure, it's only a river."

"What's in the field?" Mary asked.

"Only muck, by the look of it," said Emer. She coughed again.

"What grows in the muck?"

"It used to be barley," said Tansey.

"And it might still be barley."

"Bend number three coming up!"

They'd walked past the field and there were hedges on both sides again and trees that touched each other over their heads, so it was dark and even darker again. Mary could hear the branches rasping and complaining in the wind. She was glad she wasn't alone, although she liked the sound and she always had.

"We used to think that the people who were gone lived up in these trees," Emer told them.

"You mean, people who'd died?" said Mary.

"The very same," said Emer. "The noise of the leaves – that was them whispering, and the like."

"Was that you?" Mary asked Tansey.

"Was what me?"

"Were you up in the trees when Granny was a girl."

"I was not, faith," said Tansey. "I'd have more to be doing than shaking around in trees."

"I was only asking," said Mary.

"And I was only answering," said Tansey. "But I'll tell you. It's the right kind of sound, all the same."

"The leaves?"

"The leaves."

"It's nice."

"It is."

"Bend number four!" said Scarlett. "I remember!"

"We'd better be quiet from here on in."

"Is Mammy asleep?!"

"I am not."

"Sorry!"

"No harm."

"Shhhhh!"

Mary could smell the cows. It wasn't an old or a distant smell, as if the cows were in a field a good bit away. It was a new, fresh smell, like the cows were right beside—

She screamed.

There was a face, hanging, right in front of her.

"Ohmygod!"

It was a huge face – huge eyes staring at her, and a tongue that was going to—

"It's only a cow," said Tansey.

"Well, what's it doing there?!" said Mary.

"And why shouldn't it be there?" said Tansey. "The poor ol' thing is only looking over the hedge."

They heard Emer snort, as if she'd suddenly woken up.

"It was exactly the same as when I was a girl," she said.

"And me!" said Scarlett.

"Shhhh!"

"And the exact same place."

"It can't be the same cow surely," said Emer. "Or can it?"

"Not at all," said Tansey. "Sure, the creature would be nearly a hundred if it was the same."

"It must have learnt the habit, so," said Emer. "The cows passed it on, through the years."

"Cow to calf."

"Maybe it's the ghost of a cow."

Mary could feel the cow's warm breath on her face.

"No," she said. "It's real."

She looked at Tansey.

"Do you breathe, Tansey?"

"No, thank God," said Tansey.

They heard Scarlett laughing.

The cow's big face was still hanging there, in front of Mary. She could see much more now, the hedge and the rest of the cow behind it. So, the face made sense. It had become funny, even sweet. The big eyes were beautiful. Mary could see the moonlight in them, two tiny moons, one in each big eye. She patted the cow's nose.

"He's kind of soft."

"She," said Tansey. "That beast's a girl."

"Oh, all the best beasts are girls," said Emer.

Mary patted the cow again, and the cow pressed its face closer to Mary's hand. Saying hello, welcoming her – that was what it felt like.

"Off we go," said Tansey – she whispered.

"Bye, cow," said Mary.

She had to walk around the cow's head, because the cow hadn't moved. She could hear her mother whispering ahead of her.

"Bend number five!"

Mary and Tansey still held hands. Tansey's hand was

very cold but nice – soft and gentle. Any time Mary was about to step into a hole or trip on a stone, Tansey's fingers seemed to squeeze hers slightly, to warn her. The trees were gone from over their heads, so she could see a bit more. There was pale, weak light that seemed to be behind the hedges, as if it couldn't climb over and light the lane properly.

"Bend number six!"

"Nearly, nearly there."

Mary had never walked into a farmyard before. She'd never been on a real farm.

"Bend number … seven!"

But, still, she felt she knew where was going, that she'd done this before, that the smell – cattle, hens, machinery, oil, dogs – was very familiar.

She almost bumped into her mother.

"Sorry."

Her mother, with *her* mother still on her back, had stopped at the gate to the yard. Mary stood with Tansey, just as a cloud shifted in the sky above and the moon lit the yard, just for them.

"Oh, Lord."

It wasn't a nice surprise.

The gate was hanging from the post; it hadn't been closed in years. The yard was empty. There were huge weeds, like bushes, growing everywhere. There were no animals, and no noise. The place was silent. But the biggest, shocking silence was at the far side of the yard.

The house.

The roof – the straw thatch – was gone. There was nothing in its place.

They wouldn't go any nearer. The moon was out, and it told them that there was no glass in the windows. Nothing shone, or winked. The front door was gone, it was just a door-shaped hole. The weeds would be in there too, inside the house, breaking through the floor, climbing the walls, grabbing the banisters, pulling the place down to the ground – where it had started nearly two hundred years before.

"That's a surprise."

"And not a pleasant one, faith."

"'Twould make you want to cry."

"I am crying!" said Scarlett.

"Me too," said Mary.

"Good girls," said Emer. "Cry for us all."

She patted Scarlett's shoulders and Scarlett let her gently down to the ground. Emer was standing now. She put her arms around Scarlett's waist.

"We'll cry," she said. "And then we'll stop. Because it's only a house."

"She's right," said Tansey. "'Tis a pity but nothing else, and nothing more."

She stood at the gate and sobbed – although ghosts weren't supposed to. And Mary understood: it wasn't the old house they were crying about. Not really. It was for themselves they were crying, their endings and starts. There were four of them tonight, but who knew how many there'd be tomorrow night? Two of them had lived in that old roofless house. Two of them now lived in a different house, a house with a roof, in Dublin.

Things changed.

Four of them stood together, holding one another. But only three of them actually lived.

They cried, and they stopped.

"No greyhounds either," said Emer.

"You never liked the greyhounds," said Tansey.

"Ah sure, I liked them enough," said Emer, "now that they're gone. I'd prefer to see them here than not see them here, even though they did frighten me. But, sure."

She pulled Mary to her, and hugged her. "That's life."

It was three in the morning when they got back to the car.

"Tired?"

"Yes."

"No."

"D'you know what?" said Emer from the back of the car, as Tansey helped her with her seat belt. "I'm as tired as it's possible to be. But, still and all, I'd love to have a whiff of the sea. So, Scarlett, my lovely daughter—"

Mary looked at her mother's smile as it got bigger and took over her face.

"Yes, Mammy?!"

"Can you get the sea to come to us?" Emer asked. "Or would it be easier just to drive to the sea?"

Scarlett started the car.

"Let's drive!" she said. "It's on the way home!"

"Will there be corners?" asked Tansey.

"Yes!" said Scarlett. "And bends!"

"Hear that, Emer?" said Tansey. "There'll be bends."

"More bends," said Emer. "They'll be the death of me."

Mary heard the two old women in the back laughing as her mother did a U-turn across the empty road.

"Courtown!" said her mother. "How does that sound?!"

"I always liked Courtown."

"And Courtown always liked you, Emer."

"Did you ever bring me to Courtown?" Emer asked Tansey.

"The once," said Tansey. "We did. With your father. Before James the Baby – sorry, James the Man – was born."

"Did we have a nice time?"

"Oh, we did. We had a great time altogether. Although, now, you threw your sandwich at a seagull."

"Did I?"

"You did."

"Did I hit him?"

"You did," said Tansey. "Right on the head. But no harm. He picked up the sandwich in his beak and flew off with it, not a bother on the creature. And you ran after him, wanting the sandwich back. And you fell, and the squeals out of you! Half of Wexford thought the English were after coming back."

They laughed and giggled, and stopped. Mary turned

and saw that her granny was asleep. Her head was leaning against Tansey's shoulder. Tansey smiled at her, and Mary smiled back. Then Mary looked in the rear-view mirror, to see her granny leaning against nothing.

"Weird."

"What is?!"

"Nearly everything."

Emer missed all the corners and bends to Courtown – it took about forty minutes. But she woke just as Scarlett stopped the car, in a car park right in front of the sea.

"Oh, look."

The moon was a silver line on the water, all the way across the Irish Sea, to Wales.

"It's like a magic road."

"Too straight for my liking."

They sat there for a while, then got out of the car and walked across a little bridge, across another narrow road, and up a few steps – Mary helped her granny up the steps – so they could see the sea properly and smell it, and feel the wind. It was chilly, but not too bad. Mary and Scarlett had their jackets, Emer was wearing her dressing gown under her coat – and ghosts don't feel the cold.

They sat on the steps, side by side by side by side – Mary with Scarlett, with Emer, with Tansey.

"I always loved the smell of the sea."

"And the sound of the waves!"

"That too."

"Boring," said Mary. "I'm being cheeky."

"Care for a swim, Emer?" said Tansey.

"Ah no," said Emer. "Enough is enough. I was never mad about the water. Just the smell of it I always liked."

She coughed again, for quite a while.

"I can't swim, sure," she told Tansey. "I never could."

"It's never too late to learn," said Tansey.

"Ah, it is," said Emer. "And I'm not interested in swimming. But that now—"

She pointed back at the amusements arcade, the Golden Nugget, behind them.

"That was only brilliant."

"What was?" said Tansey.

"All the stuff in that place," said Emer. "The one-armed bandits and penny-rolling machine, and the machine that told your fortune, even though it was only a cod. The noise and the lights. Scarlett loved it too. D'you remember, Scarlett?"

"Yes!"

"Pity it's shut."

"We could wait for it to open."

"No," said Emer. "It's fine. We'll go in a minute."

"Alright."

Emer pressed her mother's hand.

"Is dying a bit like that?" she asked, very quietly – she didn't want to upset Mary. "The afterlife and the rest of it. Is it noise and whirring lights?"

"It's nothing to be frightened of," said Tansey. "Do you understand me?"

Emer looked at Tansey.

"Yes," she said. "I think I do."

They cuddled up together. And, beside them, Mary and Scarlett cuddled up together too.

Tansey spoke, to all of them.

"We'll never be far away, you know," she said. "Even when you can't see us any more."

Scarlett had started to cry. Tansey leaned across and put her arm around her.

"When you want to see your mother, look at your own face in the mirror," she said. "Or look at your Mary's face. Or Mary's daughter's face. Emer will be in there. You'll see. And so will I. And so will you. And so will Mary."

They were all crying again. But it was fine – it was nice.

It was great.

"I don't have a daughter," said Mary – she wiped her eyes and nose.

They started laughing. So did Mary. *I don't have a daughter*. It was the funniest thing they'd ever heard.

"You will some day," said Tansey. "Or you might."

"That's weird too," said Mary. "I'm not being cheeky."

"I want to go back to the hospital now," said Emer.

And that made them cry even more.

"Would you like to come home with us, Mammy?" Scarlett asked.

"Are you talking to me, Scarlett?" said Emer.

"Yes," said Scarlett. "Of course."

"It's a bit confusing," said Emer. "There are three mammies sitting in a row here."

"Well, you're the mammy I was talking to," said Scarlett. "Would you like to come home with me and Mary?"

"I'd love to," said Emer. "But no. I think I'm better off back in the hospital."

"Oh, Mammy."

"I'm grand, I'm grand. And I've had a lovely time. I met my mother – imagine."

She laughed – and coughed.

It was getting colder – or it seemed to be.

"I'd love an ice-cream though," said Emer. "A cone."

"Oh."

"Me too," said Mary.

"It's four in the morning," said Scarlett.

"I can help there," said Tansey. "I'll get the ice-creams. There's a shop back across with a big cone outside it. That'll be the place for the ice-creams."

"You can go through the door!"

"I can."

"Cool."

"But," said Scarlett. "How will you pay?"

"You'll give me the money and I'll leave it there, beside the ice-cream machine. It'll fill their day when they come and open the shop, and us back in Dublin. 'Who put the money there?' they'll be asking."

They walked slowly to the car. Tansey went ahead, straight to the shop on the other side of the car park. She stopped in front of the door, shimmered, and disappeared.

"Ohmygod! That's so cool."

Scarlett and Emer leaned against the car and looked at the sea while Mary waited for Tansey to come back out through the shop door.

But Tansey didn't come through the door. It was still dark but Mary saw something on the roof of the shop. Four white things came out of the chimney, followed by – she saw it now – two hands and two arms, the elbows, and a head and shoulders. It was Tansey and, for a second, she looked like the Statue of Liberty, holding up four white flames instead of one.

"Ohmygod."

Tansey stepped on to the top of the chimney, then off it, and she glided down the roof. She seemed to slide right down the wall, to the ground. Mary saw her walking towards the car.

"Why did you go that way?" Mary asked.

"I could come back out through the door because, well, I'm not real, I suppose, and that's what I can do. I'm not solid when I don't need to be. But the ice-creams are solid, for a few minutes anyway, till they melt. So I couldn't get the ice-cream through the door. Only up the chimney."

"They're not covered in soot, are they?"

"Only my one," said Tansey. "And I won't be eating it. I only have it to keep you company."

She handed out the cones and they sat on the bonnet of the car and looked back at the sea for a while, until Emer was ready to go.

"That was lovely," said Emer. "Imagine. My mother stole an ice-cream for me."

"I didn't steal it, Emer," said Tansey.

"Ah, but it's the thought that counts," said Emer.

By the time they got to the hospital, daylight was pushing the night away. Scarlett parked the car at the front door, just as it started to rain.

There was no one standing outside the hospital. It was like the whole world was still sleeping. Mary liked it. She'd never been up this late – this early – before.

"Come on, Mary!" said Scarlett.

She opened her door and got out.

Mary quickly understood: they were going to leave Tansey and Emer alone together for a little while, before Emer went back in to her bed. She opened her door and ran after Scarlett, to the bus shelter.

They stood there, and listened to the rain tapping the plastic roof.

"It's cold," said Mary.

"Yes."

"It's sad."

"Yes, it is," said Scarlett. "But it's – I don't know – wonderful too. Isn't it?"

"Yes," said Mary. "But it's still sad."

"I know."

Back in the back of the car, Tansey and Emer said nothing, for a while. They looked out at the rain, until there was too much rain and nothing to see.

"They'll get wet," said Tansey.

"Good enough."

"Ah now."

They laughed, but only a little bit.

"The feel of the rain," said Emer. "On your skin. You only appreciate that when it's about to be taken off you."

"Not everything's great, you know," said Tansey, "just because it's going to stop. You would never eat your turnips. You always said you hated them."

"And I still do."

"You won't miss them, so."

"I will not."

"See now."

"But I'll miss hating them."

"Were you as cranky as this all your life?"

"I was, of course."

"Good girl."

They sat quietly for a while. The rain ran down the windows. Then it slowed – it made no sound – and stopped. The early sunlight filled the car.

"Nice and warm now," said Emer.

"Are you still frightened, Emer?" Tansey asked.

"I am," said Emer. "A bit. But that's natural, I suppose. Is it?"

"Yes."

"I'll put it this way," said Emer. "I'm a little bit frightened but I'm not really worried any more. Does that make sense?"

"It makes a lot of sense," said Tansey.

Mary and Scarlett saw one of the back doors open – the door on Emer's side. They ran over to the car, to help her out. Emer stood, and looked up at the sky.

"That's a grand day now," she said.

Mary looked into the car. Tansey was still sitting in there.

"Are you not getting out?"

"No," said Tansey. "I'm grand in here."

"Oh," said Mary. "Okay. Will I close the door?"

"Do."

Mary grabbed the door handle.

"But before you do," said Tansey. "There's one thing."

"What?"

"Remember the leaves."

"Is that all?"

"That'll do," said Tansey. "Good girl. I'm that proud of you, Mary. Shut the door now."

Mary closed the door. She had to slam it. She tapped the glass.

"I didn't mean the slam," she said.

They heard Tansey through the glass.

"You're grand."

They got the wheelchair out, and went into the hospital. They made their way to the lift, and slowly up to Emer's ward. They helped her take off her coat and dressing gown.

Emer looked very tired.

"I'm ready for the bed," she said. "I must look like I've been up all night."

"You, like, *have* been up all night."

"Well, there you go. Give me a hand here, girls. I'm a greyhound of a girl but, God, the bed's after growing since I climbed off it last night."

They helped her climb on to her bed. She lay down, slowly, carefully, and she muttered.

"Good back, nice back, don't give out and crack."

Her head sank slowly into the pillow.

"We have lift-off."

Mary sat beside her, up on the bed, and they chatted for a while, with Scarlett sitting on the other side.

"What big eyes you have, Granny."

"All the better to eat you with, my dear."

Scarlett wet her finger and dabbed the tip of her mother's nose.

"Now why in the name of God did you do that?"

"There was a little bit of ice-cream there, all dried up!"

"Ice-cream?" said Emer. "Oh, yes. Was that tonight?"

Mary pointed at the bright day on the other side of the window.

"Last night," she said.

"We're wild," said Emer. "Aren't we now?"

As she spoke, her eyes closed, and she slept.

Mary and her mother waited, then they slowly slid off the bed. They leaned across and both kissed Emer's forehead.

Then they left.

When they came back out to the car the hospital was getting busy, and Tansey was gone.

Mary woke up. She was in her own bed, at home. The light was off but the curtains were open. So she could see her mother, and her father, and her brothers, standing beside the bed.

She sat up and rubbed her eyes.

"You slept all day," said her mother.

"Did I?"

"Yes."

Her mother sat beside her.

"Your granny's gone," she said.

"Gone where?" said Mary.

Then she understood. Her granny had died.

She hugged her mother, and her father. She even hugged her brothers. The room was full of sobs and snorts and sighs.

Mary hugged Scarlett again. She could feel Scarlett's tears wetting the side of her face.

She let go of Scarlett and got out of bed. She went across to her window. Scarlett went with her and they both looked out, at the night and the swaying trees. The street lights lit the leaves and, when a car went by, the headlights seemed to make them dance. They watched the leaves bob and the branches sway.

Scarlett opened the window, and now they could hear the rasping of the leaves. They could imagine they heard voices and laughter as people they couldn't see moved among the leaves.

They cried and they smiled.

"What are you doing there?" Mary's father asked.

"We're listening to Granny and Tansey," said Mary.

"Who's Tansey?"

"We'll tell you in a minute," said Scarlett.

They stood there, holding each other, for a while longer, crying.

Then Mary thought of something brilliant. She let go of her mother and wiped her nose.

She spoke.

"I want a greyhound," she said.

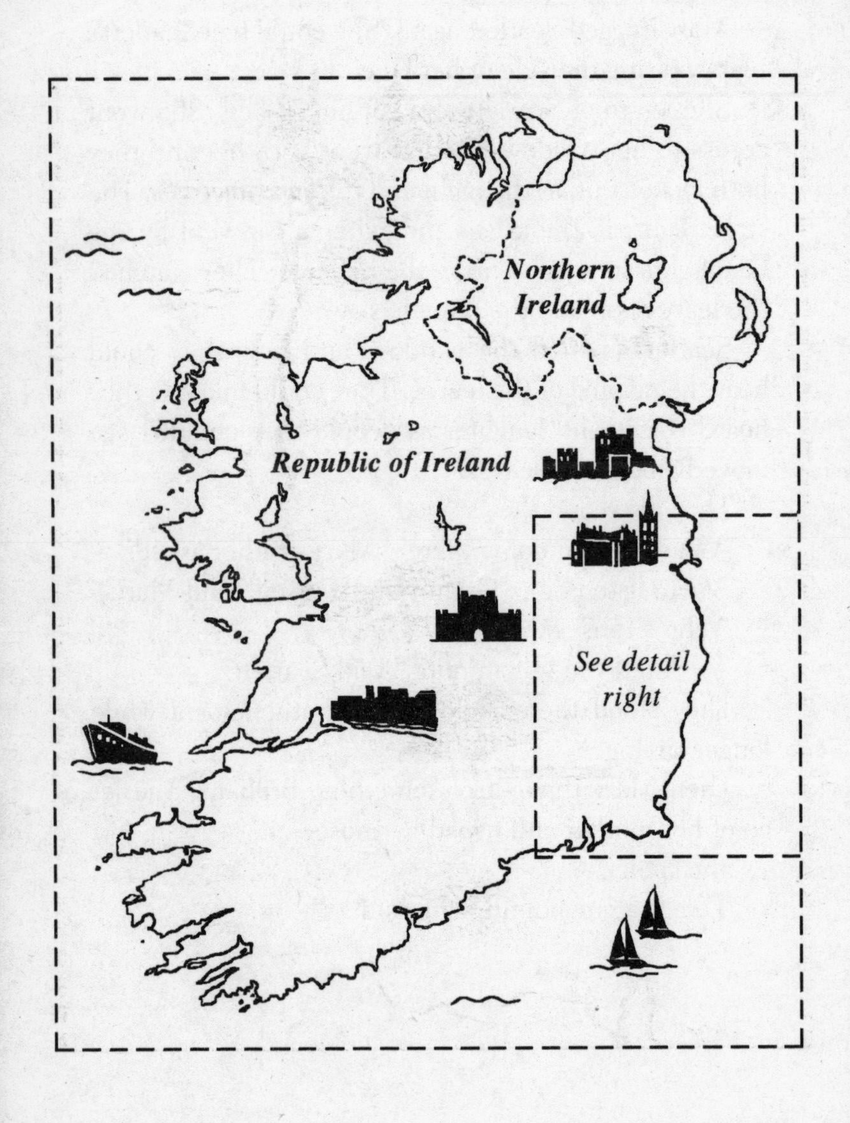
Northern Ireland
Republic of Ireland
See detail right